# THE LATECOMER

# The Latecomer

DIMITRI VERHULST

*Translated from the Dutch by David Colmer*

Portobello
BOOKS

Published by Portobello Books 2016

Portobello Books
12 Addison Avenue
London
W11 4QR

Copyright © Dimitri Verhulst, 2013

Originally published in Dutch as *De laatkomer* in 2013
by Uitgeverij Atlas Contact, Amsterdam

Translation copyright © David Colmer, 2015

The translation of this book is funded by the Flemish Literature Fund
(Vlaams Fonds voor de Letteren – www.flemishliterature.be).

Flemish
Literature
Fund

A CIP catalogue record for this book is available
from the British Library.

1   3   5   7   9   10   8   6   4   2

ISBN 978 1 84627 567 8 (trade paperback)
ISBN 978 1 84627 598 2 (ebook)

Typeset in Bembo by Patty Rennie

Printed in the UK by CPI Group (UK) Ltd,
Croydon CR0 4YY

www.portobellobooks.com

MIX
Paper from
responsible sources
FSC® C020471

I'm crossing the Styx and taking: a tube of toothpaste
(just for a joke) . . .

★

Although it's completely deliberate, night after night, I
loathe shitting in bed. Debasing myself like this is the
most difficult consequence of the somewhat insane
path I've taken late in life. But holding back in my
sleep could only arouse the suspicions of my carers.
If I want to continue to play the role of a senile old
man, I have no choice but to regularly soil my nappies.
Because that's what this is: a role. I am nowhere near as
demented as those around me believe!

I

The acid in my urine has started to eat away at my buttocks, which is not the most pleasant sensation I've experienced. The salves and ointments Aisha and Curvy Cora smear between my cheeks while swooning over the tasty body of the Kukident adhesive cream rep, who comes to this home to peddle his wares, provide no relief at all. But as I've said, under no circumstances can I cut incontinence from my script. Just imagine what would happen if they suddenly discovered that for several months now I've been successfully feigning dementia! That for weeks and weeks on end I've been babbling nonsense or wobbling apathetically in my chair when really I am still quite capable, for example, of explaining things like contemporary political issues. The health service would feel robbed and take me to court. The staff, especially the female staff of Winterlight Geriatric Care, would feel exploited, as if their integrity has been compromised, and happily bash my brains in. The pity my children still manage to feel for me would be transformed into boundless shame. And my wife (the bitch), assuming she survives me (and she will), would scatter enormous amounts of bird feed over my grave to keep the pigeons shitting on my memory.

So, no, I don't have any alternative. I've burnt my bridges, there's no going back. Once in the old gits' home, always in the old gits' home. I knew what I was getting myself into. But that doesn't change the fact that, of all the tasks that come with the plausible simulation of a completely senile senior, incontinence is the one I find most difficult. Many times I've lain here at night with tears in my eyes as I squeeze my guts out in bed. No one can accuse me of a lack of willpower these last few months, but sometimes, lying in my own sticky filth, I've begun to question the whole enterprise. Those were the rare moments, the ripe moments, when I asked myself, 'Is it worth it? Haven't I gone a tad too far?'

But now the solution has presented itself. To my relief.

The vast quantities of pills the nurses here shove down our throats will have something to do with it, but last night I didn't wake up once. Slept like a corpse. Which meant I wasn't able to force myself to treat our health-care providers to a big fat turd.

However . . .

Curvy Cora rushed into my room this morning, as hurried as ever (unbelievable how that girl stays so plump when she's so fidgety), opened the curtains and cried, 'Rise and shine, Désiré! It's a brand-new day and everything's going your way!'

That's when I felt it. To my surprise, I'd shat the bed! Spontaneously and without any effort! Hallelujah! My metabolism had taken over the task that was proving too onerous for my will.

'Désiré, did you hear me? Time to get up!'

I exclaimed, 'Mother, Mother, the cows need to calve!' And Curvy Cora had to laugh; Curvy Cora can laugh beautifully. A lot of fat people have beautiful laughs. She said, 'The cows have already calved, Désiré. Shall we go to the cowshed later and have a look? After breakfast? And we'll take some stale bread to feed the birds in the garden, they're already warbling away for you! But first, I need to freshen you up, so the girls in the dining room will all say how handsome and well-preserved you are again.' And she tossed my legs up in the air and dipped her flannel in a warm bowl.

'*Impropria est ut salutaret aliquis qui est cacas*,' I cried. Not altogether appropriate, perhaps, for someone who was going senile. But I still whooped it out, as happy as the child I was meant to resemble more with every passing day.

*Impropria est ut salutaret aliquis qui est cacas*: it is unseemly to greet someone who is just having a shit. Erasmus.

Whereupon, Curvy Cora replied, 'So, Désiré, you've impressed me now! Is that the Bible?'

It really was a brand-new day and definitely going my way.

Clean and naked and smelling of disinfectant soap, I lay on the bed. Curvy Cora assessed my wardrobe with a pretence of solemnity and bellowed at me. That too is a difficult aspect of premature admission to an old people's home. The horrific, never-ending shouting. The staff assume for convenience's sake that all old

4

fogeys are as deaf as a post and after a few years on the job their vocal chords are like steel cables. Some geriatric workers are so used to bawling and bellowing that conversation at an acceptable volume is completely beyond them. They yell constantly at their partner and kids too. Lovingly, most of the time, but still.

And so Curvy Cora shouted, producing a hazardous level of decibels. 'Today we're going to put on our best suit, Désiré! And you know why?'

'Whazzat?'

'We're going to put on our best suit today!'

'Oh.'

'And you know why?'

'Uh-huh.'

'Why, Désiré?'

'Yes.'

'Because it's our birthday! And how old are we today? Do you know that?'

I could get very annoyed at her for her bizarre habit of speaking in the first person plural. Was it something she'd been taught during her training? If so, I was very curious about the philosophy behind a rule like that.

'Seventy-four, Désiré! Isn't that a grand old age!'

With my seventy-four years, I'm definitely one of the babies at Winterlight Geriatric. Everyone under the age of eighty is seen more or less as a hard-luck case. A person who may have received a respectable dollop of grey matter from Mother Nature, capable of deciphering the most complicated codes or storing all kinds of useful information, but never thought to check the use-by date.

Take Etienne Thijs in room 18. He's under seventy-five too. An egghead his whole life, a professor of biology, pioneering research into antibiotic resistance, and now as loony as a baboon. He puts his clothes on back to front and keeps a scrapbook with pictures he's cut out from *Miaow!*, the cat-lovers' monthly. Sad. And meanwhile his wife, who's a thousand times thicker but fit as a fiddle mentally (where have I seen that before?), has found another bloke, a retired butcher. When she comes to the home to visit her husband, she brings her lover with her. Professor Thijs doesn't even realise, and for that we can be truly thankful.

Winterlight's craziest character isn't Prof. Thijs, though, not by a long shot. That honour is reserved for Walter De Bodt, more than a century old, bald and bony, an archipelago of liver spots, often to be seen sitting in a wheelchair in his khaki-coloured ex-army pyjamas. (I'd like to honour him with the nickname Camp Commandant Alzheimer, but when there's next to no one apart from yourself to talk to, a nickname doesn't get you very far.) The only person Walter De Bodt respects is the head of geriatrics, the 'care manager', as he is tendentiously known, who Walter invariably greets with a rigid right arm and, if his false teeth are properly inserted, a cry of 'Heil!'

Having to relive your younger years is seldom something to crow about.

And if a person in their seventies who has lost their mental moorings is *not* seen as a hard-luck case, well, it's because they think you had it coming. You're under suspicion of not having eaten enough fatty fish when you had the chance. Or nuts. You preferred TV soaps to books with complicated plots, you drank so much alcohol you pickled your brain, you turned your nose up at crossword puzzles and never read foreign-language newspapers. You were the kind of person who preferred to avoid any kind of mental strain, who couldn't find the energy to keep up with new technology. You are fully and solely to blame for your own dementia! That's the way some people look at you.

That's how my wife looks at me. When she visits. Something she, fortunately, does less and less.

It's my first birthday in the home and I'm in the mood. Hip, hip, hooray for me. OK, to cut costs and reduce stress, I will have to share my party with any other residents who happen to have had their birthdays in the last fortnight. Mostly that works out at two or three birthday boys or girls to make a simultaneous fuss of, and if one of them's turning a hundred, you're guaranteed a journalist from the local newspaper will show up to cover the happy event and photograph the celebrated centenarian. The alderman responsible for births, deaths and marriages will also drop by. He'll give a short speech (always the same one, but with a senile audience that's the least of his worries), present the brand-new hundred-year-old with a flowering pot plant on behalf of the mayor and all his fellow councillors, wish him or her many, many happy returns, scoff a piece of cake, press the flesh of any eligible voters, and disappear. Residents who are only turning ninety-eight are significantly less fascinating for this alderman (a Christian-Democrat, but I doubt that makes a difference) and the celebration of a seventy-fourth birthday means nothing to him at all. An even better opportunity for the alderman to put in an appearance is when the chance of immortalising four generations in one go has the regional press photographer scurrying our way yet again. Such a moving portrait: a quivering bag of bones with a freshly dropped great-grandson on his lap.

Today, praise the Lord, there is nobody in the birthday batch whose clock is just ticking over to three digits, so the alderman can amuse himself with more useful matters. You won't hear me complaining. The way he sometimes dares to look at me, I get the feeling he's the only one who's seen through my little game. The only one who knows I've still got my full complement of marbles, that I'm taking everyone for a ride. It's a feeling I have, nothing else. Pure intuition.

Curvy Cora: 'Look at you, Désiré, all squeaky clean

again. Off to the dining room!' Ninety-four decibels.

With a patronising, 'Why don't we put today's birthday boys next to each other at the breakfast table?' she wheels me round and parks me in the spot that belonged, until very recently, to Rosa Rozendaal. What little hair Rosa had left pointed in all directions. At breakfast, she'd shove a slice of bread into her mouth like a boxer replacing his mouthguard and mutter to herself.

In Rosa Rozendaal's old spot and right next to Camp Commandant Alzheimer. The camp commandant has already launched his attack on his tasteless white sandwiches, though not without dunking them in his mug of weak coffee first.

I look into his glassy eyes and say, 'How do you like the butter? Good, isn't it? Made from the body fat of Jews! A real delicacy!'

This kind of talk always rekindles Camp Commandant Alzheimer's former glory. It seems to remind his empty head that it once contained thoughts. He parrots, 'We'll have more jobs, wider motorways, better railway connections!' then stabs his knife deep into the butter to demonstratively smear a thick, flabby layer on a new slice of bread. But the man shakes so badly the butter's soon stuck to everything except his knife.

I whisper, 'You don't recognise me, do you?'

Now he looks uncomfortable. It's the uncomfortable look of a dementia-sufferer furiously rifling through

9

his memory in search of something that's almost certainly not there anymore. The look I have spent hours rehearsing and have now mastered.

'You don't recognise me anymore? Look closer! It was the last winter of the war, that cold winter . . . You shot me dead and threw me on a pile of bodies! No? My face doesn't ring any bells? Oh, well, I understand. You killed so many. You can't be expected to remember all those faces. Still, I was one of them. And I've come back. Risen from the dead, out of the ovens. To blight your old age. To stick a garden hose up your ancient arse and turn on the tap until clean, clear water's gushing out of your nostrils.'

The healthcare sector isn't just underpaid, it's also understaffed. And so it takes a while before someone arrives to smother the camp commandant's piggy squeals with a comforting gesture and a quick sedative.

'Walter, come now, there's no reason for you to scream the building down just because you've dropped some butter on the floor. That's really nothing to worry about, dear. But next time, just ask us if you want some extra butter on your sandwich. That's what we're here for, after all, isn't it? Is that a deal? OK?'

Of all my birthdays, none began as promisingly as this one, the very last.

★

I'm crossing the Styx and taking: a tube of toothpaste
(just for a joke), a stray Joseph Roth quote . . .

*

All the world's best ideas mature slowly, like extra-tasty, crumbly cheese. My plan to fake dementia was also built up one step at a time, sometimes without me even realising it. I can't identify with any certainty just when and where it began but, if I was forced to pick a single moment, I'd say it was that afternoon – when exactly? – two years ago, two and a half maybe, at the pétanque club. Because, yes, I enjoyed a game of boules with my mates. I found it very relaxing. Not my wife. She thought pétanque was an activity for loafers, a game that had been invented by the tax department to maintain levels of alcohol and tobacco consumption, and she often treated me to statements like: 'When it comes to raking the moss out of the lawn you're always feeling a little peaky, then suddenly you're energetic and sprightly enough to make a fool of yourself tossing balls around a sandpit. I have gone down on bended knee a hundred times, Désiré, begging you to please come with me to Sanders Furniture Emporium to look for a new cupboard for the tea towels. And it's always your blood pressure this or your bad back that; you're never up to it. As far as you're concerned, that cupboard for my tea towels can wait forever. But if it's to go pétanqueing, you never have a problem. Not with your blood pressure, not with your back, not with anything . . .'

I've long stopped sticking up for myself in the face of my wife's tirades. I'm one of the many, perhaps millions of silent men who armour themselves against their wife's vagaries with a shield of indifference. It took me years of patient practice. At first I resisted every unjustified accusation. With a clear conscience, I would insist that I never drank more than three glasses, that during our entire marriage I had come home drunk a maximum of four or five times, which, as I now realise, was probably far too infrequently for my mental health. What's more, I used to have the gall to try to correct her ridiculous view of things. I would say, 'Listen here, for starters you don't play pétanque in a sandpit, it's a bit more elevated than that.' But as my youth and hair receded, I learnt to be insensitive to her verbal fusillades and kept my replies to myself. By the time the mortgage was paid off, the house surrounded me like a prison. But I boosted my self-respect with acts of resistance: it was her venom versus my detachment. We both stubbornly held our positions and grew old together unromantically, even surviving friends whose relationships were loving. When the mayor of our town honoured us in the town hall on the occasion of our golden wedding anniversary, I felt guilty thinking of those magnificent couples who had been torn apart much too soon by cancer or a fool with a gearstick, and deluded myself that I was right to accept the mayor's tribute, but only as something I had earned through bravery and self-sacrifice.

Since people in these parts treat proverbs as dogma and unthinkingly assume that where there's smoke there *must* be fire, there can be no doubt that at least some of them believed my wife when she once again began to complain that I was an incorrigible drunk. It's true that I drink two glasses of red wine a day. Drink? Drank! Two. Sometimes, as an exception, three . . . in the evening after dinner. It was a habit I developed some-time in my mid-thirties and it stuck. I almost said 'and it *has* stuck', but the senile shufflers in an old folks' home

13

aren't granted much pleasure after dinner: organising evening activities is the last thing the staff are interested in; they just pump everyone full of stupefying concoctions so they'll doze off in front of the idiot box like good boys and girls.

I haven't needed to renounce my small, hen-pecked pleasures entirely. Here in the canteen I can order a glass of red now and then in the daytime. When I'm sitting in my armchair with an addled, depressed look on my face and Curvy Cora comes to give me a little professional cheer, rubbing my shoulders and saying, 'Oh, Désiré, you're sitting here all quiet and alone without so much as a drink. If you're not careful you'll get dehydrated. Should I go and fetch you something?' I'm brave enough to ask for a glass of wine. That's allowed. It's the cheapest plonk, of course, a watery concoction I sip expressionlessly, more grape juice than wine, and you'd need to guzzle a whole case of it to counter the effect of the medication.

'Here, Désiré, look. Your glass of wine. Enjoy. But make sure you don't get drunk and start singing, huh? The other residents might think the dance afternoon has come early.'

. . . Ooh, cootchie-cootchie-coo.

It was divine providence, by the way, that I happened to be sitting in the canteen with a glass – unfortunately still dirty – of Château Migraine the first time my wife came to visit me in this home. The day after my admission. I can still see her walking in with a basket of fruit, a TV-commercial smile and a box of chocolates. Of course, I pretended not to know her.

'Look who's come to see you, Désiré, your wife!'

'Whozzat?'

'Your wife!'

'Oh . . .'

Once the image of her incorrigible husband had fully sunk in, she screeched theatrically in the hope that the nursing staff would lend their compassionate and militantly feminist ears to her chorus of woes as an unhappy housewife.

'I can't believe it, Désiré. You're drinking again already! And then you act surprised you're going bonkers!'

Which inspired me to declare, 'Sit down next to me, Camilla, and have one yourself. It's on me. I've got a tab here!'

Needless to say, this reunion and my remark insulted her deeply, not least because my wife isn't called Camilla, but Moniek. And, given that I have the good fortune of living in a country where wives generally keep their maiden names, not Moniek Cordier, but Moniek De Petter. A beautiful name . . . to see on a headstone.

(Incidentally, according to her passport she's not

Moniek, but Monique. She thought spelling it like that was way too stuffy and didn't suit her at all. People who consider it necessary to change their name . . . Need I say more?)

But I'm getting ahead of myself. I was still, as I recall, explaining when and where my idea for the role of a lifetime emerged and that it probably began to take shape during a game of pétanque. More specifically because of something Roland, my regular partner, said . . .

Of all my buddies, Roland has always been the most modern. He was the first in my circle of acquaintance to ignore the apocalyptic warnings about all kinds of tumours and warm up his meals in a microwave. The first to know that, unlike an LP, a CD did not have two playable sides. The first to acquire a mobile phone and praise its advantages. The one who sent text messages and, as if that wasn't enough, sent them to the people who were meant to receive them. The first computer I ever saw in real life was in his living room. While the rest of us were still pondering the possible effects the Internet would have on our private lives, he'd already done a course and cobbled together a club website. Roland did his banking online, booked trips from his armchair, took digital photos of our games and put them on his Facebook page (without asking us if we were OK with it first). He'd long switched to buying his boules and equipment on auction sites. That kind of guy, someone who keeps abreast of everything, who knocks your boule out of the solar system, then says, 'There's something I have to tell you . . .'

A lot of Roland's most outrageous stories began with, 'There's something I have to tell you . . .'

And this was definitely something worth telling: an Australian had put his whole life up for sale on the Internet! His *actual* life. All he *had* and all he *was*. His wife wasn't included in the price; she'd left him, you see, and that was the reason the nutcase was flogging his entire existence to the highest bidder. You *did* get his crappy job in a carpet shop in Perth, along with his friends Melanie and Em. His hobby (skydiving), his three-bedroom house, his Jet Ski, his barbie and his sneakers (Converse, size 8) were all part of the package. The guy was completely disillusioned and wanted to wipe the slate clean. And what was possibly even crazier was that there were already more than a hundred registered bidders and the price of his life had shot up to almost two million Australian dollars!

The fantasy of just-selling-off-your-whole-existence amused us no end and, discussing it, we tried to imagine what it would be like to associate with someone you didn't know at all but had just purchased as an ex-lover. Or going up to someone and saying, 'Pleased to meet you. I just bought you as my dad. How's Mum? Oh, she's dead? Whoops, didn't know that, it wasn't in the ad. How long now?'

That afternoon I didn't play my best. Unable to concentrate on the match, I kept fantasising about that crazy Aussie escape artist. I can still hear Roland shouting, 'Hey, Désiré, wake up! It's your throw! You're staring into thin air as if you've gone completely senile!'

And how they laughed. Especially when I, incomprehensibly, threw my boule in the wrong direction.

★

I'm crossing the Styx and taking: a tube of tooth-paste (just for a joke), a stray Joseph Roth quote, the wondrous memory of an ardent kiss I never got . . .

★

People my age don't have Facebook or other sociable computer whatsits to cheat loneliness; no, we bump into each other in *real life* with gruesome frequency at funerals, the most natural occasion for us to maintain contact with our diminishing outside world. Towards the end of my run-of-the-mill middle-class existence, there was a deceptive ease about the way I pulled on my black overcoat, ready to accompany another old acquaintance to his or her final resting place. After a while, I caught myself driving to the crematorium on autopilot, the way I'd driven to the library for work all those years.

Can you believe I sometimes miss it, standing in a cold church to say goodbye to another lost buddy? The theatrics of it all. It's undoubtedly the only performance in which the supporting roles are more sought-after than the lead. Arriving in the morning while the bell tolls for someone else, the old crones and geezers gather in front of the portal, some of them still dumbstruck at attending yet another funeral before their own. The laconic sighs, 'Here we are again, huh?' And then the inevitable questions. 'How old was he? . . . Seventy-nine? . . . Oh, that's much too soon to have to go in this day and age, but yeah, what can *we* do about it?'

Yes, what could we do about it?

Nowadays we always think of ourselves as too young for the worms or the chimney. Rounding the cape of eighty should be a piece of cake in those regions where the majority of the population has access to modern medicine. Even cats make it into their twenties with relative ease these days, thanks to the massive improvement in the quality of tinned cat food. And as a cat, you'd have to be very old-fashioned indeed to still fancy a fat little free-range mouse, twitching its tail just in front of your jaws. But we old-age pensioners still smash the television set, howling with rage when it shows a twenty-something, jauntily lit by the halo of his own dreams, a wag in a suit, with the self-confidence of someone who's just bought his second car, claiming that he has lost all faith in the social-security system, that he's not participating in the strikes against the right-wing reforms because he has no desire to contribute to the pensions of all those who clocked off forever at the age of sixty-five. And you feel him biting his tongue almost in half to avoid undiplomatically adding, 'If those bald-headed bastards are still fit enough to practise their various hobbies, they can just as well get a job.'

From the start of each requiem we, the pensioners, know in our hearts that the body in the coffin being slid from the shining limo is old. Irrevocably old and worn out. As old and worn out as we ourselves. But because a mad roll of the dice has kept us this side of dying, and half embarrassed with regard to the deceased, we say that he or she has been robbed of a few beautiful years. Justice is a human concept, in nature it is nowhere to be seen. Unless the lamented has been laid low by a filthy, painful disease; then we reduce our late friend to the poor wretch they were during the last phase of their life and express our gratitude to death, their saviour.

We bow to the person who is laid out, splash a few drops of holy water over the coffin lid perhaps, offer our condolences to relatives who don't have a clue who we are and wonder what on earth our significance in the life of the demised might have been. We then seek out our regular, much-too-hard pew, on which we, fighting drowsiness, undergo the litany. How grateful we are when incense obscures the bier and we are finally free to cough ourselves out of our boredom; glad to be able to stretch our stiff legs by fetching a host from the altar or a holy card with an accompanying portrait and saccharine verse. We listen to the obligatory funeral hits, which, though subject to the whims of fashion, seem keen to assert in extremis that the deceased had been afflicted by extremely poor taste. After that, all the hymns are sung and the bodily remains disappear through the big gate, hoopla into the big dark hole of eternal forgetting, amen.

Winterlight funerals aren't as bound by ritual. At least not for those whose funeral service takes place under this roof, those who have been left over, discarded and erased from other people's memories even before they became the filling for a burial plot. The priest rattles through his prayers in a tearing hurry before an audience that sometimes consists of just one token nun drummed up for the occasion. No funeral march, no tolling of bells, no elegies for a life whose details all have forgotten, the only traces of which are to be found in the odd medical dossier. A hearse drives up to the rear of the building – the goods entrance, where they also keep the rubbish containers – loads up the dead body and quietly drives off again. A room has become available, the cogs keep turning.

No, give me a chat in the town square with the other hangers-on after the funeral service, dredging up semi-consoling memories. During what was ostensibly the last funeral I attended with my mental faculties fully intact, we were standing under the plane trees when a member of our regular clique let slip, 'Next time we're standing here together in our black raincoats, it could very well be for Rosa Rozendaal!' I wonder still if it was clear from my face how distraught that made me.

Rosa. Rosa rugosa. Rosa nitida. Rosa villosa. Rosa Rozendaal.

It had been more than fifty years since I had heard someone mention Rosa Rozendaal. To be honest, I had given up hope of ever hearing her name cross anyone's lips again. I thought she had taken off long ago to live somewhere else, where life was that little bit more gripping, and with a man, of course. I presumed she had borne children who had all been university material, and she herself, after a fulfilling career, had thrown herself into grandmothering a following generation.

Rosa Rozendaal . . . I was sixteen and she was the first girl I ever danced with, at one of the very first parties my parents let me go to. The Albatross Party

Centre, the Saturday of the town fair. Earlier in the evening, local hero Victor Wartel had won the annual bike race and his victory was doing wonders for the turnover at the bar. And a little later accordion trio The 3 Jacksons, world stars in territories just under and just over sea level, played some racy adaptations of Fats Domino songs, 'Muskrat Ramble' . . . and other things that drove that year's crop of spotty adolescents wild.

Suspecting me of being any kind of lady-killer would be a mistake; it was Rosa who flouted the custom of the day by asking me to dance. And that made me the luckiest person in the entire northern hemisphere, if not far beyond. Rosa: I had hardly dared to look in her direction, but now I was out on the dance floor with her. Not even the gods could understand what I'd done to deserve it. Not the gods, and certainly not me. I felt an urge to apologise to the crowd of boys glowering at me through the smoke of their Belga cigarettes. Do I need to spell out that I hadn't missed my calling as a dancer? I could keep time, sure, but that was all. Still, I was apparently good enough for her to dance with me for one more song. Something wild and devilish, rock 'n' roll, a new wind that was warmly welcomed by dancers of my inept ilk as its rhythms made it possible to compensate for a lack of technique with commitment alone. She was feeling a bit hot, she said. She wanted to step outside for a breath of fresh air and asked if I'd go with her. Up to this point, she'd done all the preparatory work. An enterprising character. But now it was up to me. There was no point in being coy about it, I knew what I had to do. No girl alive asked a boy to step outside with her for no reason. And definitely not when they'd just been dancing together. But when we got outside I didn't do anything. I just stood there for a while next to her. Just standing there. Thinking up the most pathetic questions a boy could come up with on such a glorious occasion. Where she went to school, if she liked going to school, what kind of job she was thinking of doing later, and, for Christ's sake, if she had any idea if she wanted to have kids and, if so, how many . . . It was effectively my first party and I wanted to show her that I was a gentleman, that I had more than one thing on my mind. Of all the great secrets that are peculiar to the female of our often disgusting species, I was convinced I knew one: namely that women have a horror of men who make their move too quickly and too directly.

Meanwhile Rosa had cooled off (*you should have warmed her up, you idiot*) and suggested going back inside, those three Jacksons were still playing. I realised immediately that I had put my heart and soul into squandering a chance that had been presented to me on a golden platter. As for Rosa, what must she have thought? That I was a member of the limp-wrist brigade? That I didn't think she was pretty enough? That I was on the verge of choosing to further my studies at the seminary – I was already studying Latin after all? No idea, but the bird had flown, never to return. In the months that followed I saw Rosa several times in the company of a youth who could grow a proper moustache and the sight always pained me to the roots of my teeth. But after that she simply vanished. Never to be seen again. If someone had told me she'd moved abroad, I would have believed it instantly.

There are unavoidable phases in every human life when, sometimes for a reason but often by chance alone, we find ourselves returning to a pivotal moment in our existence and wondering what would have become of us if we'd tipped just that little bit further in one direction or another. And it goes without saying that these meaningless, almost masochist musings have repeatedly led me back to Rosa Rozendaal and the two of us standing together in the car park of the Albatross Party Centre. In my thoughts I've followed every possible route my life could have taken that day, but it's a fruitless exercise that can only lead to the false glorification of a thwarted destiny.

But a name can boomerang straight back in your face after decades and decades.

'There's something I have to tell you: next time we're standing here together in our black raincoats, it could very well be for Rosa Rozendaal. I've heard

26

she's suddenly got a lot worse. Upstairs, you know. Arteriosclerosis. They had to put her in a home, the poor thing, as young as she is.'

And with that, all the stories were exhausted and everyone went their own way: to trim a hedge, knock up a chicken run or spray the patio clean with a pressure washer . . . We wished each other the best and dispersed, knowing our paths would not converge again until the next funeral.

★

I'm crossing the Styx and taking: a tube of toothpaste (just for a joke), a stray Joseph Roth quote, the
wondrous memory of an ardent kiss I never got, bread
crumbs . . .

★

It was one of those glorious summer days that drench
the boggy edges of the North Sea far too rarely. Our
children had come to visit and we were sitting in the
garden, where they had once (it feels like yesterday)
swung back and forth in their innocence and boredom,
building forts. Hugo, our son, was there with Lisa, his
third floozy, and the whole raucous teenage gang the

two of them had cobbled together from various relationships. Also present was our daughter, Charlotte, who seemed to have gone about things better and still lived in harmony with her first real flame, Pascal, perhaps because they'd had the good sense not to reproduce. My wife, who had an opinion about every possible subject, put it down to impotence.

'No, of course, it has to be. Why else would our Charlotte stay childless? And it's probably his own fault too, with those tight jeans he's always wearing. They're not just ugly, they kill off your family tree as well!'

Even in the most inappropriate moments, she had no scruples about pushing the conversation in the direction of the sperm bank whenever Charlotte dropped by.

This summer afternoon the mother hen demonstrated her aversion to subtlety by suddenly pulling out a strip of pills. This was just after serving up the Melba toast with cream cheese and radish.

'Hey, does anyone have any use for these? Erection pills! They were prescribed for Dad, but he only ever thinks of himself and refuses to take them! No one? Not you, Pascal? No? You sure? Hundred per cent? . . . I'm just going to throw them away otherwise . . .'

You can imagine the awkward silence that descended over our garden as everyone tried to avoid looking at me.

ooo

29

What preceded this scene? Behind my back the serpent that answers to the name of Moniek De Petter had gone to her GP to complain about her feeble love life. After returning, she had prattled away archly, 'I talked to Dr Dumoulin about your problem and you know what? He gave me this: Levitra! It's like Viagra, but not as well known. But measured in inches it's just as effective. Plus, a less familiar brand name has the advantage of nobody thinking of what they should be thinking of if you absent-mindedly leave them lying around . . .'

Wives have been thrown off bridges for less.

Of course, I felt humiliated in front of my children, who were at least tactful enough to change the subject. (Hugo launched into a discussion of Crete, how delicious the food was. And cheap too, all things considered.)

More than just rude, my wife's public attack on my pride that afternoon was completely unjust. At the start of our marital relations, in the early sixties, Moniek successfully convinced me that I was a base animal, solely because I occasionally had the temerity to suggest a position other than the one we employed for all our love-making. The frequency of my desire was on the bestial side too as far as she was concerned. Twice a month was wild enough for her; after all, we weren't rabbits. During her two pregnancies there was no sex by definition, it would have been improper. The thought of the baby getting my 'doodle' in its little face the whole time, yuck!

To safeguard myself from her accusations, I began leaving all initiative to her, though I realised this wasn't doing my sex life any favours. I can't say with any certainty if she ever once had an orgasm. To be honest, I don't think so (asking straight out was not an option), but I gave up reproaching myself on that account long ago. Of course, as a young man I had dreamed of a more flourishing future in the erotic arena and I suffered in silence from the disillusionment of my far from heavenly marriage. Never did I seek consolation for this stolen happiness in the arms of others. I could have forgiven myself for it. Easily. And I would never, ever have confessed my infidelity; there's such a thing as a right to a little peace and quiet. But Moniek's frigidity was all I knew and there was no way I could draw on that to gain the necessary confidence in myself as a lover. I should also admit that nobody ever presented themselves. My libido was slowly snuffed out and if I'm honest I'll add that I was glad to be rid of it. It wasn't any good to me anyway. Even before we'd reached forty, you could count the sexual contacts between us per year on the fingers of one hand.

Bizarrely enough, my wife's passion awoke once I had completely embraced my celibacy. By that time we were sleeping in separate rooms: for appearance's sake we claimed it was because one of us snored and the other tossed and turned, and the broken nights weren't doing either of us any good. All of a sudden she started knocking on my door more and more often and had to learn the brutal lesson of accepting the very same 'no' that had razed my male pride to the ground long ago.

'Rabbit!' I would shout, but a sense of humour had never been one of her attributes.

Once we'd grown ugly, she was suddenly in the mood for love. Come off it. No, she was an extremely unsporting loser and took revenge by humiliating me in front of others. My bedroom door has remained, figuratively speaking, permanently closed. What happens or rather doesn't happen inside has never been anybody else's business. But now that she had falsely ridiculed me like this, I felt a rising urge to tell my children that it was a miracle they had been conceived at all, given the prudishness of the refrigerator I was married to.

I looked at her standing there, the bloody hypocrite, holding that strip of erection pills.

But one of us had to outsmart the other and silence was a better tactic.

Especially now, with the plans for my final offensive ripening apace.

So, yes, I held my tongue. My speciality. It was essential that I not spoil the garden party.

We were planning on informing the children that this might be the last time we would sit together as a family in this garden. The reason was simple: the upkeep was too much for me. It was taking me longer and longer to mow the lawn and the toll it took on my lower back was getting worse and worse; I had started to let nature run its weedy course, and the hedge clippers hadn't left the garden shed all year. Growing old is no fun, but being old is worse. Besides the garden, there was the exterior woodwork, which needed painting biennially, if not annually. Plus all the other countless jobs that come with owning a house and garden and were now beyond me. A tap that needed descaling, a sagging door, a drive belt that had come off in the washing machine . . . They became colossal tasks.

'You're lazy! You give up much too easily!' So said my wife. Who else? 'Just look at next door's garden, how beautifully that's maintained. This year Michiel trimmed his hedge in the shape of a swan. If a Japanese tourist happened to pass by, he'd stop to take a photo of it straight away. And how old do you think Michiel is? Three years older than you!'

Moniek saw the struggle against physical deterioration as a competitive sport.

'Did you see Lucienne? She could hardly walk! You'd think she'd make more of an effort to lift her feet up. I told her, "Lucienne," I said, "if you don't show a little more courage in resisting old age, you'll be dead and buried before you know it! At our age you pay a terrible price for laziness of any kind at all . . ." Talk

33

about ungrateful, I should never have raised the subject. The look she gave me . . .'

What Moniek was less keen to broadcast around the neighbourhood was that she too was not immune to the ravages of time. Her elephant marches around the house with a vacuum cleaner were taking longer, and more often than not she had to interrupt her wars on fluff and spiders to catch her breath. On the bike to and from the baker's she had started to wobble, and for an old-age pensioner with osteoporosis a single smack against the tarmac can be the beginning of the end. A broken hip is our greatest fear.

The process had been long and painful, but we were ready to sell the house and move into a flat in town. She had fought hardest against what she saw as collaborating with decrepitude. One of those little flats people use to adjust to the regime of an old folks' home was cowardly capitulation . . .

I should have been relieved when Moniek finally admitted to being ready for something smaller in town, where there'd be a range of shops close at hand and fewer windows to clean. For her, the decisive event had been a fall in the bath: she didn't hurt herself badly but had to lie there soaking for three hours until I heard her cries for help and was able to liberate her from the tub she'd stepped into independently, but couldn't climb back out of. Yes, that made the idea of a flat with modern conveniences like a shower suddenly more appealing. But greater than my joy at never again needing to paint an outside wall or exterminate moles was my growing revulsion at having to move somewhere new with this woman. Despite the demands it put on my stiff muscles, this garden had been my haven for all these years, somewhere to be alone for a while. It was where I fed the birds and while I did so I was happy with my place in the universe. In a flat I would have to sit even closer to my wife, chin-to-chin. If we were lucky, we'd find something with a balcony big enough for a drying rack and a flowerpot. I wasn't looking forward to putting our house up for sale, having estate agents and potential buyers tramping through and quibbling over every penny, the slick conversations with the leeches at all those banks, men who were ready to squeeze you dry if you requested a simple bridging loan, the maze of legal paperwork to negotiate, having to apply for a new telephone number . . . And on top of all that rigmarole, Moniek again, who wouldn't be able to bring herself to clear out the attic and say a definitive goodbye to the thousand and one things she hadn't given a second glance for ages but still considered essential, guaranteeing that the flat would immediately be rendered uninhabitable by piles of junk. Like many women, my wife suffered from chronic shoe-itis: she was incapable of walking past a shoe shop without her interest

35

being aroused. As a result there were one hundred and forty-nine pairs of shoes in our wardrobe, of which she was unwilling to discard a single pair. Add in the scientifically established fact that in nine out of ten cases this condition is accompanied by handbag-itis, and you can rest assured that every available square metre in one of those flats would immediately be taken up by leather goods. I only had to close my eyes to hear her trotting out her full repertoire of clever remarks:

'Why on earth should I get rid of shoes or handbags to save space? It's not as if you can take your lawn-mower to the flat with us. Or your chainsaw. Your vice isn't going to be any use to you either. Work it out! How many shoeboxes fit in a lawnmower?'

No, I couldn't bear all that. Let alone romantic-ally bickering over the colour of the new curtains, the design of the bathroom, the pattern on the kitchen tiles . . . . thanks, but no thanks! I had already decorated one house with Moniek and I hadn't found it romantic back then either.

The vol-au-vents had been served, the mashed potato too. (For Charlotte, who couldn't stomach vol-au-vents, there were cheese croquettes.) And Mother, that epicentre of all that breathed and clipped coupons, said, 'Kids, we've got something important to tell you! Will you tell them, Désiré?'

'Huh? What?'

'Will you tell them?'

'But what?'

'You know, what we were going to tell them. The news, of course!'

'The news?'

'Yes, the news!'

'Can't it wait till after dinner?'

'Why do we have to wait? Isn't the dinner allowed to know what we're going to do with our lives? Come on, out with it. The children will start worrying it's something terrible.'

I said, 'All right, then, if you insist . . . Hugo, Charlotte, we have to solemnly inform you of something: namely, that your mother has just bought her one hundred and fiftieth pair of shoes!'

My son-in-law, Pascal, laughed long and hard, but he was the only one.

Moniek then delivered the News herself: 'Your father is no longer up to washing out paintbrushes, so we're looking for a little flat in town where he can park his bum in an armchair and fossilise!'

I was pretty sure I could see deep disillusionment clouding her eyes, simply because our children weren't putting on a show of grief at having to kiss the parental home goodbye. She had hoped for theatrical reactions, sorrowful pantomimes that originated in a carefree childhood whose memory they would cherish forever. But Hugo and Charlotte's verdict was terse and unanimous: 'You should have done it long ago. Making Father get up on a ladder with his bad back to paint the window frames or clean the gutters is just cruel . . .'

And then, a shriek out of nowhere, 'Tart! I forgot to buy a tart!'

Nutritional experts agree that breakfast is the most important meal of the day, but for Moniek it's dessert, consisting preferably of a tart with a crisp base, butter cream and fruit smothered in jelly. And a blob of cream, of course. Her forgetting to buy a tart for this afternoon was a very worrying sign: if I wasn't careful she'd get dementia before I did!

'Moniek, please, don't worry about the tart, we've got more than enough to eat. What's more, anything we don't scoff today, we don't have to worry about losing again tomorrow in the gym.' (Lisa, the daughter-in-law: someone who always knew her precise body weight. The sight of a potato instantly made her think of potassium.)

My son-in-law must have been delighted at the prospect of not having a slice of tart shoved under his nose. The poor sod had let himself be coerced into eating three big helpings of vol-au-vents. And no less than five portions of mash. Because, even if he was already over the crest of forty, 'A young man like you needs to eat well!'

When he refused a sixth helping, Moniek stared at him in bewilderment. 'Finished already! Son, you're a disappointment. You know what they used to say in my family when I was little? Bad eaters, bad workers! That's what they said.'

But we were discussing the tart. There had to be a tart no matter what. Some people had such funny ideas: fancy suggesting that a meal in the garden with the whole family didn't need to end with a big mouthful of pastry!

'Désiré, get your bum into gear and go for a drive to get us a nice tart! Then your legs might remember what it's like to move for once!'

I returned one and a half hours later.

'So, Robinson Crusoe, where have you been? And you went off without your phone too, so we couldn't even reach you. Our Charlotte, the poor child, started biting her nails she was so worried. And that's no life for a woman, walking around with ratty little chewed fingernails. And all because of you!'

'What do you mean, where have I been? I had to go to the shop, didn't I?'

'Of course you had to go to the shop. But did you really need to take an hour and a half to buy a tart? Or are you going to tell me they still had to bake it?'

'A tart?'

And I plonked a shiny new toaster down on the garden table. 'It's a good one. In terms of value for money, the best! A two-year guarantee.'

I could see our children's panic in the looks they exchanged. They knew what they were in for.

My show had begun. The first act.

★

Mother Goose was sitting in her armchair, the armchair that was always covered with blankets to keep the cushions clean, waiting for the start of the soap opera she had already been addicted to for twenty-three whole seasons, and began jabbering at me:

'Shall we play a game?'

Moniek had never been one for games, she found them too frivolous. But she probably thought she was clever enough to pull the wool over my eyes.

I said, 'What game?'

'A memory game! I'm going to market to buy!'

'Are you going to market?'

'No, that's the name of the game. I'm going to market to buy. For instance, I say, "I'm going to market to buy a first-aid kit." And then it's your turn and you can add something, but you have to remember what I'm buying too, because then you can get it for me. So you say something like, "I'm going to market to buy a first-aid kit and three pairs of socks." And so on. Ready?'

I said, 'I don't want to go to market. Just go by yourself!'

Her TV show was starting on its eleven billionth episode, something to help her in her struggle against despondency.

*

On paper it seemed easy enough: I would more or less crumble away like one of those lonely bluffs you see in Westerns. Slowly but inexorably, with something resembling grandeur, I would blur and gradually disappear in the mist I myself was discharging. Degenerating so gently that in the end the existential night would fall almost unnoticed. If there's such a thing as the art of living, then there must also be an art of dying. But my craving for results was so fierce I had to be careful not to overplay my hand. What's more, I had reached a fair age and was *already* slipping into the pathetic state all elderly people have to contend with sooner or later. There's no need for me to list the skills I had already lost by the time I started on my last and greatest adventure. They were enough to make you weep, my irreparable ailments, that much was certain. My grave-bound roller coaster was already going fast enough. The milepost of no-longer-being-able-to-trim-my-own-toenails

41

had shot by long ago. My life, which had largely been a disappointment, was coming to an end anyway. It wasn't as if my little plan was cheating the planet of my presence in any significant way.

Strangely enough, I had decided to play a role in the piece I feared most: dementia. For thirty-eight years my memory allowed me to carry out the profession of librarian flawlessly – and that in an era in which card indexes were gradually being replaced by the first, monstrous computers and people, as a result, mostly had to rely on the completely biodegradable database in their heads. If you gave me a subject or an author's name, I'd spit out a whole series of titles. Without wavering. If somebody mentioned 'Louis Albrechts', for instance, I could instantly add *'Town and Regional Planning in Scotland'*. And here I'm citing a book that wasn't borrowed once (because for goodness' sake, who, in our provincial dormitory town, was going to be interested in how the Scots planned anything at all?) but was simply fixed in my brain because I saw its spine every day. There were probably thousands of names, titles and subjects like that, books I could summon up at the drop of a hat, a modest talent that justified my exist-ence in the eyes of many a lazy student uninspired by the theme of their essay or presentation. A memory like an elephant, people said. But I lost my glasses at least ten times a day and my car keys just as often, and the names of people who lived up the street went in one ear and straight out the other. And if I didn't arm myself with a shopping list, I was sure to come home with either the wrong groceries or far too few. My absentmindedness is legendary, inasmuch as there is anything legendary about me at all. More than once I've managed to put a lasagne in a cold oven. I've killed two, yes *two*, car engines by filling up with diesel instead of petrol, and at family get-togethers the kids still tell the story of how we once left for a holiday on the Lac du Bourget, our favourite destination, and I didn't realise until we'd reached the French border that I'd forgotten to hitch the caravan to the tow bar. More often than not, Moniek would seize on situations like this to exclaim, 'There you have it. It's come to this: Gorbachoff's Syndrome! . . . The booze and nothing else . . .'

The ninny!

My suggestion that they too, in their capacity as passengers, could have noticed that we weren't pulling the caravan made no difference. No, I was the driver, the one who was constantly looking in the rear-view mirror, and therefore solely responsible for the extra kilometres we had to cover because of my negligence . . .

Anyway, I wasn't entirely relaxed about my forgetfulness either and took my worries to a neurologist friend of mine. What could it be that allowed my brain cells to juggle dusty quiz-winning encyclopaedic facts while being totally impervious to frequently used telephone numbers, birthdates, the names of friends' wives and the names of my brother's grandchildren, even though he never shut up once he got onto the subject of those little descendants of his? For years now, a myriad of life's petty details had drifted through my consciousness without leaving any kind of impression. Add in the aggravating genetic circumstance of having witnessed the dotage of no less than two of my grandparents: my mother's mother saw tomahawk-brandishing Indians dancing around the deathbed she clung to for dear life; she wept and sweated and pissed the sheets with fear, to the exhaustion of the nuns, who tied her down and tried to cure her with prayer. That was more than enough to convince anyone that their degeneration was predestined and every hiccup of forgetfulness, a first hesitant sign. But my buddy and well-known noggin researcher reassured me with an apt metaphor. He said, 'If you're searching for a name and feel like you're rummaging through a file in vain, you're fine. The essential thing is that you have that file at your disposal, that you possess a file in which you have stored all your names and information. With Alzheimer's, or dementia in general, the whole filing cabinet's gone.'

That image was very useful. Convincing the outside world that my whole filing cabinet was rotting away was now my task.

But rot has a rhythm of its own and too much haste would betray me.

It's known that dementia is generally diagnosed much later in people who have a tendency to be absent-minded. I, too, would have to live with the fact that my inner circle refused to be perturbed or even surprised by my follies. Of course it was fear I had read in my children's eyes when I came home with a toaster instead of a fruit tart. But a few minutes later they were entertaining each other by recalling the countless other stupidities I had committed, with the story of the caravan trotted out yet again and still good for spasms of laughter.

The dazed look on Dad's face, remember?

In this initial phase a slight increase in the frequency of my slip-ups seemed the best strategy. And I have to admit to feeling an old, half-forgotten pleasure, usually reserved for toddlers and surrealists: the simple amusement of turning reality on its head and lifting all kinds of things out of the rut of their everyday context. Instead of putting out the rubbish bag, I put the laundry basket out on the street. (Where it disappeared, much to the fury of Mrs De Petter.) I fed the fresh bread to the birds without waiting for it to go stale first, showered with my socks on, put the dirty dishes in the washing machine. (Not recommended: it makes a hellish racket, which is then drowned out by shrill shrieks when your wife sees her parents' bone china dinner service being smashed to smithereens by a washing programme designed for cotton shirts.) I put tomato soup in the coffee thermos, hung teabags in the toilet bowl, turned the heating up to maximum on the rankest summer afternoon . . . Until something in Moniek's tiny mind finally twigged that there might be more going on than simple absent-mindedness. And to better present that joyous moment, I need to return quickly to one of the first nights of our marriage. The third or fourth, I think.

Specifically the night I dared to pass wind under the sheets in the presence of the woman who had just promised before God and our monarch to be mine for better or worse. It wasn't a vulgar fart. I mean, I didn't start squeezing extra hard to show off my flatulent talent. It wasn't a stink-bomb that would cause permanent damage to the bronchial tubes of all who sniffed its odours. No, just a common-or-garden fart, the kind that is born ingloriously in its billions every day through the ventilatory orifice of humans and animals alike, something that couldn't possibly have the power to drive a wedge between husband and wife. None the less my *parp* had barely sounded before my wife was beside herself with rage. Who did I think I'd married? A barbaric, ill-mannered freak? Someone who was used to sleeping in a pigsty?

It was impossible to calm her down. Moniek leapt out of bed and rode her bike back to her parents', where she spent the next two nights. I never found out what

46

she told her family about me. She must have told them something, because they can't have been expecting to see their married daughter back home in the middle of her honeymoon.

('Mother, help, I've married a farter!')

When she returned – as if from a period of quarantine and furious to boot because I hadn't made the slightest effort to get her back – I had to promise never again to lower myself to such bestial practices in her presence. And I now know that acceding to this demand meant squandering my last opportunity to make something of my life. After all, she was the one who had left me; I was in the right. I could have divorced her with my head held high. But I took her back and, like a shameful creature, began a life of surreptitious windiness.

Until this moment: the dawn of a new era!

A fart and, I can assure you, one that more than made up for all the strangled exhalations of the previous decades. A cannon shot that would have delighted me even more if it had reeked to high heaven as well. Unfortunately one can't have everything in life, and definitely not at the same time.

I waited for an unprecedented scolding, an eruption of fury that would be heard up and down the street, to the great amusement of all our neighbours. But no, not a thing. Moniek didn't even react to my sonata for bombardon. She wept. In silence, the way I was supposed to break wind. She wept her tears and I knew my

47

triumphal procession had begun. She had lost her last shred of doubt. She knew that soon she wouldn't have a husband to nag and harangue. She'd have the house to herself and could die in it alone.

If she didn't feel sorry for herself now, then, well, who would?

*

I'm crossing the Styx and taking: a tube of toothpaste (just for a joke), a stray Joseph Roth quote,
the wondrous memory of an ardent kiss I never got,
bread crumbs, greater solace than a good Berliner ever
offered me . . .

★

In Azalea Street the appearance of a police van is still
an event that gets tongues wagging. I'd almost say, a
festive event! The siren doesn't even need to crank out
its angry lament, just having the vehicle drive down
the street quietly sets the dogs barking and has the local
gossips taking up their positions behind their curtains.

49

A story is on its way, preferably one concerning the suffering of others. The scandalmongers rub their hands, for once life seems to have been plucked straight from TV. Hip-hip hooray!

The last time the gendarmerie came calling in this neighbourhood was to inform the Vanderelsts at number 54 that their daughter hadn't survived the trip back from the disco.

I can't say with any certainty that the neighbours expected equally exciting news when two police officers parked their van in our drive, but it was remarkable how everyone, despite the late hour, suddenly needed to empty the letterbox or sweep the pavement in order to move a few steps closer to the mystery and uncover the reason behind the arrival of the boys in blue. Out of the corner of my eye I saw Felix from number 47 inspecting an imaginary problem with the side of his house and getting the shock of his life when he spotted my dishevelled self in the back of the van, a place usually reserved for people who have just been arrested. He immediately hurried back inside, no doubt to inform his family. I felt the eyes of the whole neighbourhood on me. The buzz of assumptions and suppositions.

*'Is that the cops at the Cordiers'?'*
   *'Nothing bad, I hope.'*
   *'That's weird, they've got Désiré with them.'*

'Désiré? Is he hurt?'

'Not that I can see. Maybe he's been up to something. Being taken in for questioning.'

'Désiré? Up to something? A respectable old plodder like him? I really can't imagine what.'

My wife too must have thought back to the pitiful fate of the Vanderelsts after seeing the blue glint of the silent yet menacing lights flashing over her pan of cold stew. Maybe that was why she turned deathly pale and came rushing out, terrified of that one piece of information that would make the past turn into something she'd imagined.

What could have happened to me? A brief recap. She knew that just after lunch I'd gone into town to buy some new books. For Moniek, a shopping mall was heaven on earth, but there was no question of her retail Valhalla including a bookshop. It was one of the four trillion points on which we were polar opposites, so it would never occur to her to come along and I had a free hand to go and satisfy my craving for reading material. 'Off to buy books, you say? I'll leave you to it, then.'

My intention of going to a bookshop must have come as both a surprise and not a surprise. *Not*, because I'd always been mad about reading, of course. On the other hand my urge to buy books surprised her now because she couldn't reconcile my rediscovered appetite for literature with the decline in my mental faculties. For a moment she must have thanked her lucky stars she had deferred telling everyone about my failing memory. A straw of hope to clutch at, the hope that she might have been mistaken about my condition, that it had only been a temporary setback. My head had gone on holiday and come back in one piece, ready to knuckle down again, as keen as ever, with a pile of books.

I really did come home with that pile of books. Or rather, the police were so kind as to deliver the books when they brought me home. But unfortunately for Moniek, the titles couldn't confirm her hope that I was at least in remission: *How I Run Marathons*; *A God for Daily Consumption*; *Willy Snotter and the Order of Ninety-Seven Broomsticks*; *A Beautiful Garden in All Seasons*; *1001 Home Repairs*; *Original Casseroles* . . . and another ten or so works of a similarly literary bent. A considerable chunk of our family budget, by the way. Paid with a smile.

I was no stranger to the bookseller; around a quarter of the titles on our bookshelves were from his bookshop. He must have scraped together at least a couple of family holidays from my belletristic gluttony. There was no question of his not knowing my literary obsessions and he must have had his reservations about my sudden interest in casseroles, origami and garden furniture. But it's not every day a bookseller gets a visit from a dementia sufferer and times were hard for everyone, including small businessmen, so he seized the opportunity to make one last killing at my expense and sold me the most disgusting garbage. Also with a smile. Knowing full well that I wasn't all there as I bought these cack-handed publications. Even more disgusting: this man who, through the contents of my bookshelves, had been granted some degree of insight into my intellectual values, stooped so low as to deliberately overcharge me.

Of course I was tempted to drop the mask and confront the dirty money-grubber with his dishonesty and lack of ethics. It would have been worth it for the look on his face: his gob gaping open with surprise when I told the leech that I was only feigning dementia for a laugh, to see how people reacted. But this pleasure – mostly reserved, I presume, for investigative journalists and undercover policemen – was one I had to forgo. No matter how tempting it was to step out of character, just for a moment.

With the help of my shopping trolley, I then transported this load of books to a clothes shop. A trendy place, with blaring music and an industrial interior. The two women behind the counter gaped at me as I walked in. An old coot with a shopping trolley. I was the most ancient pillock by far to ever set foot in their hip establishment. Their joke of the week embodied: that was me, it was obvious. And they were already smirking in anticipation of the moment I figured out that I'd wandered into the wrong shop and realised this wasn't the place to buy something like a tweed cap or a walking stick, but oversized jeans that hung halfway down your bum. It was only when I actually started to rummage through the summer collection that one of the two approached me (the ball bearing in her extravagantly exposed navel didn't shock me in the least, but I did find it quite ugly) and quacked, in the duck-like tones that unfortunately characterise the majority of the female members of the garment sellers' guild, 'Can I help you, sir? Are you looking for anything in particular?'

I gave her a glazed look, at least that was what I hoped I was doing, grabbed a random piece of clothing and asked if I could try it on. The piece of textile concerned could most deferentially be described as a casual shirt, albeit one without sleeves and decorated with a loud print of an English slogan referring to an activity healthy couples usually perform on a mattress. In all her youthful vanity, the girl probably assumed I didn't speak a word of English.

Her colleague remained where she was behind the cash register but had followed the entire conversation and was now having visible difficulty in suppressing an undoubtedly ugly laugh. A laugh that would soon erupt like the contents of a ripe boil.

I took a few more shirts and jeans into the fitting

room and twisted myself into all kinds of clothes in psychotic hues that I, as a father, would never have tolerated on my children.

The next step was crucial and essential for moving my life's final project up to the next level.

I left my own, age-appropriate clothing on the rack and exited the fitting room decked out like a pathetic carnival character. (Tautology!) The girls abandoned all attempts to suppress their guffaws. For minutes and minutes they had stood firm but further resistance was inconceivable and they burst into gales of laughter. And the laughter was as ugly as I had feared. From both of them. But before it could burst my eardrum, I had strolled out of the shop as casually as possible, still wearing all those highly fashionable, unpaid-for, brand-spanking-new rags, and completely ignoring the caterwauling of the alarm system.

I attracted plenty of attention out on the street, dressed up like a circus monkey on sabbatical as I was, but the gawking only increased when the black girl with the ironmongery in her belly button followed me out onto the pavement, pointed at me and started screeching that I was a thief and needed to be stopped.

Fine, but to my disillusionment nobody stopped me. What did the citizenry at large care if a shop full of nursery supplies for adolescents was robbed of a few yards of hideous fabric? No great loss, surely? And when it came down to it, nobody knew who I was – I could have been armed. In this part of the world, you had to do something a little more sordid to awaken a sense of civic duty. It's a miracle, really, that they still manage to sell car and other alarms at all, when you see how unanimous people are in ignoring the racket they produce.

I shuffled undisturbed to the end of the street, where I was quietly but firmly apprehended by two good cops who had evidently been informed of my approach by high-tech tom-tom. They politely requested that I accompany them back to the shop I had just left. The numerous rubber-neckers on the pavements left and right had been hoping for a dramatic denouement but were now disappointed.

And so, in next to no time, there I was, back in that very same shop. Even if my presence there didn't make much difference. With a professional composure I had thought lost to mankind, the older-looking of the two policemen scolded the teenagers playing at shop-keeper. He was willing to put most of it down to their inexperience and youthful self-obsession, and that was forgivable, but he still found it hard to believe that they could be so blinkered as to take a senile old man for a common criminal.

'You must have got a little confused for a moment,' the other policeman said to me with an unusual degree of sympathy and friendliness. Perhaps he had a grandfather wasting away under a plaid blanket in a home. Things like that hone one's empathy. 'Your clothes are hung up in that fitting cubicle. Perhaps you could change back into them? Then these ladies will put the things you're wearing now back where they belong.'

They studied my identity card. 'Azalea Street? Is that where you live?'

'Yes, I think so. Azalea Street. Yes, yes, that's it. Definitely.'

'Come on, we happen to be going in that direction, we'll give you a lift. And this here, are these your books? Did you buy them or did you just walk out of a shop with them too?'

And so I was delivered home by the police, to be reunited with my wife, who, having gulped back her forebodings of catastrophe, burst into fury at me for, once again, going out without a mobile and leaving her to wait with a saucepan full of cold stew for no good reason.

The representative of the forces of law and order: 'Could we perhaps step in for a moment, ma'am? This doesn't seem the kind of thing we should discuss on the doorstep . . .'

The entire conversation between the sympathetic officers and my wife (who began to look more and more despondent) was carried out in such a perfect whisper that I was only able to make out the word 'doctor'. And just when I thought she was paralysed by utter dejection, Moniek De Petter, my warden, shrieked, 'Dementia? Dementia, you say? If you put a glass of red wine on the table in front of him you'd see how demented he is. He wouldn't forget to drink it, that's for sure . . .'

After the police had departed, there was nothing left to peer at and the neighbours' blinds plunged back into the depths.

*

What I liked most about my performance was the restlessness of the role I had taken on: losing my grip on reality; having the feeling that somewhere, but the devil only knew where, a task was waiting to be fulfilled. I had to act like I was searching for something I wouldn't recognise if I somehow fell over it. This total detachment from our ugly, everyday sureties appealed to me. It was a lot of fun. I maundered through my days like my own stand-in, though not without assuring myself along the way that Moniek De Petter was steaming more and more recklessly towards a total nervous breakdown.

The dotard's primary occupation is flight: an urgent, desperate need to escape. With that in mind there is a bus stop in the middle of Winterlight Geriatric's garden. Completely fake, of course. I mean, no bus will ever stop in that garden or leave from it. But it's still a perfect reproduction, complete with bench and shelter, a neatly posted timetable and various notices that make the whole particularly convincing, even if none of the prospective passengers ever show any interest in them: *Road works in the High Street, delays may occur. We apologise for any inconvenience.* There is even a short stretch of road, about seven metres in total, surfaced in the magnificently smooth asphalt cyclists are so keen to get under their wheels, and a sign to a town that doesn't exist, which is also the bus's destination. The number 77. Since the establishment of this ghost connection to elsewhere, Winterlight's care workers have had to spend much less time tracking down residents who have gone missing. Nowadays when an old dear feels the urge to run away, she spots the bus stop and sits down triumphantly to wait for the next bus. After a while a nurse comes out, calls something along the lines of, 'Are you waiting for the 77, Gilberta? It's running late, pet, because of a detour or something. They're digging up the sewers in the High Street, if I'm not mistaken. Why don't you just pop back inside for five minutes? Come on now, you can have a nice cup of coffee while you're waiting . . .'

The dementia sufferers feel like their travel plans are being taken seriously, they're not pushed into even deeper confusion, and the staff don't need to interrupt their exhausting routine of pill pushing and nappy changing for another round of hide-and-seek.

The bus-stop method has been adopted from Germany and the investment is worth every penny. Each person I've seen this trick used on really has come back into the home, enthusiastically accepting the warmth and the promised coffee, and afterwards completely forgetting that they were actually determined to flee and sitting there waiting for a bus ride to freedom.

But, as I explained, this stop is at Winterlight Geriatric Care and I had to get myself signed up as a patient there first.

My clandestine research into Alzheimer's had taught me to emphasise a few key areas. Mood swings amongst others. Sitting there nice and depressive one hour, and chortling away the next, for instance at my wife's farcical hair-do. (Or the trendy glasses she'd recently purchased to convince others, and above all herself, that she was keeping up with the times. Glasses with a glaring brand name on the frame. But Moniek had always been a sucker for flashy brand names. Or products with a little label on them saying 'authentic' or 'designer' . . .)

A sleep disorder, definitely, that was another thing I had to fake if I wanted to earn my admission to dementiahood. And so I got up as fresh as a daisy when the night was at its darkest, made myself a mountain of sandwiches, treated myself to a nice bath, preferably singing, rubbed myself with lavish amounts of sun lotion and instant tan, then installed myself in front of the TV.

My orientation in time and space needed obliterating too, with long walks as a frequent consequence.

Unfortunately I was forced to cut back on these extended wanderings. Moniek grew more ashamed of me with every passing day and became terrified that I might strike up a conversation with someone who knew us. Being married to a dementia sufferer was an almost unbearable affront. The disease might occur in the best of families, but under no circumstances in ours. And so she kept me inside as much as possible, under house arrest, with the front door locked.

The neighbours' first reticent enquiries were a humiliation she felt obliged to parry with a childish excuse:

'Oh, Désiré's fine, thanks. Why do you ask? He's just very worn out at the moment. He got it into his skull that he needed to catalogue his entire book collection. You know Désiré and books. He's married to his books and he has me on the side as a mistress. In a manner of speaking, of course, you know what I mean. Anyway, he's spending so much time in his library and he's not really up to it. His leeks are bolting in the garden and he doesn't even notice, he's so preoccupied with his bookcases. Overworked, that's what he is. Nothing else. And that for somebody who's retired and should be taking it easy at long last. It's the black hole, I suppose. What else could it be except him missing his profession?'

But the residents of Azalea Street knew better. After

all, they were the ones who'd seen me walk past their front doors with a lampshade on my head.

'Hi, Désiré. Bought yourself a new hat?'

'Yes!'

'It's a beauty.'

'I have to look good when Grandma comes.'

House arrest it was. But as long as you stay alert, an opportunity is bound to arise sooner or later and one day when Moniek stepped into the back garden with a basket of wet washing I managed to slip outside unnoticed. There was no time for me to think about it or put on proper shoes. Wearing my slippers and corduroy trousers, my red polka-dot shirt and without a coat – quite tidy, all things considered – I strode out onto the street. Walking purposefully. No plan. Heading where my nose led me. Wonderful. The only thing that stopped me enjoying my escapade to the full was the self-pity that gradually overcame me as I realised how little I had given way to these impulses in the past.

I avoided the busy main roads and took streets Moniek would only search as a last resort. And as soon as I got close to the station, I knew what to do: I would board a train. The first one I saw. The destination didn't matter in the least. And without paying. After all, I had already taken one step down the criminal path. The police and I were old friends.

°o°

The first train I saw turned out to be going to Liège and that suited me just fine. During my military service I was once taken to the military hospital in Liège. Which sounds more dramatic than it was. A simple sprain. A blue, swollen ankle, nothing more. But the army medical corps must have needed people to practise on, so the sergeant had me hospitalised as a so-called precautionary measure. If this meant a temporary respite from idiotic drill exercises on damp mornings, I could only be grateful for the sergeant's decision – and that was just what it meant. I spent four days in Liège in a private room, liberated from the stench of the barracks. For purely symbolic reasons, they put a thermometer under one arm and took my blood pressure at regular intervals. And otherwise I could relax, away from the foul language and coarse stupidity the guys in my unit excelled at. No rifle range, no terrifying theory lessons on the nuclear menace. Simply four days of rest and . . . reading! From my room I had a view of the valley and the completely unknown city that filled it. I didn't set foot in its streets, apart from walking from the hospital to the train station, which I did the day the chief physician declared me fit and healthy enough to resume my defence of the country and sent me back to the barracks, but I still managed to build up a certain connection, a certain familiarity – liking, even – for all the houses and roofs I had looked out over during those four relaxed days, and resolved to return sometime after

I'd completed my military service. This city, I readily convinced myself as a melodramatic young man, had something to say to me.

I must have forgotten to keep an eye on the time and now, all of a sudden, I was decrepit. My promise to myself to return at least once to that passionate city on the Meuse had proved empty. This train could never arrive on time, but at least it could provide some slight compensation. Unless, of course, I encountered an inspector who was overflowing with professional pride, a jobsworth who would get his jollies out of showing the door to an innocent old codger who didn't have a valid ticket.

But nobody was displaying an exaggerated work ethic that day, not an inspector in sight, and three and a half hours after wandering out of Azalea Street in my slippers, I was standing on the platform of Gare Liège Guillemins, which in no way resembled the station I had left in my army uniform. A modern, architectural pearl that I had read about but was only now seeing with my own eyes. If God was a train, this station would be His cathedral.

A highly promising start to a reunion.

And perhaps that was why I abruptly changed plans, to make sure I didn't embarrass that promise. The high-speed train to Frankfurt caught my eye. Having plans wasn't a good idea anyway and could only undermine faith in my dementia. So tally-ho, onto the Frankfurt train, quick march, before the doors closed! This time I wouldn't have long to wait before someone asked to see my ticket. It was inevitable: an international train, a first-class compartment! Sparks would fly and that evening the police would once again deliver a confused man back to Azalea Street.

It proved effective: I didn't get to see Frankfurt either.

*

I'm crossing the Styx and taking: a tube of toothpaste (just for a joke), a stray Joseph Roth quote, the wondrous memory of an ardent kiss I never got, bread crumbs, greater solace than a good Berliner ever offered me, a stanza of 'Auntie Bonanza' . . .

★

Bingo, I did it! I flunked my test with flying colours, the MMS examination feared by so many of the forgetful. It was such a relief I had to restrain myself from leaping with joy in the doctor's surgery. Surely there could be no finer accolade for acting than officially diagnosing the simulator of dementia as a dementia patient! To have a medically qualified person declare him mentally incompetent and begin preparing the paperwork that will have his driving licence revoked and strip him of the ability to carry out his own financial transactions! Providing him with the properly stamped and initialled forms that will ensure he won't need to vote at the next election, and handing his wife information sheets and brochures from specialised care homes!

Champagne!

At home my wife and children had already started talking about me in my presence as if I wasn't there. Whether it was a dog or their father sitting in the living room, it no longer made any difference. Charlotte had insisted on taking me to a doctor, deploying the most artful of rhetorical devices to convince her dear mother that, no matter how much I had tended to wool-gather in the past, eating unpeeled bananas could not be taken as a sign of mental health.

Did she realise that there was already a story going around Azalea Street and its immediate environs that she was denying her sick husband proper care?

My daughter didn't need to say another word. The winning argument had been deployed and a week later the two of us were in the surgery of Dr Vancleemput, specialist in human cerebral mush.

It's difficult to say what I found the most stressful: passing my finals as a librarian or, fifty years later, failing my Mini-Mental State Examination, the last but possibly most daunting hurdle I had to clear. Because how, for heaven's sake, was I going to deceive science? How could I convince a doctor that I was a ghost ship adrift at sea?

As it turned out, more easily than I could possibly have imagined. Simply because the science was not that advanced. In my nightmares I had seen myself in a hospital with all kinds of helmets fixed to my skull with wires and pins and I don't know what else – miracles of progress that would flip the secrets of my brain onto the table like an ace of trumps. My wife had also pushed for an investigation that was more sophisticated than any that had been carried out so far. A brain scan was the absolute minimum as far as she was concerned. However, as the doctor assured us, there were lots of things a scan could show you, but not dementia! Tumours, a thrombosis, or hypothyreosis – yes, scans were extremely useful for all those things. But a condition like Alzheimer's still flew under the medical radar.

It helped that Dr Vancleemput had dropped in words like 'hypothyreosis', otherwise Moniek would undoubtedly have questioned her expertise and demanded she trot out her diplomas as proof she had actually completed some kind of training.

But still. Couldn't she have drained off a litre of blood to let a laboratory decide one way or another? Or excised a piece of flesh from a buttock to study under the microscope?

'It is possible, Mrs De Petter, that tomorrow, or next week, we'll be further advanced than we are today. People are hard at work. But at the moment neither a blood test nor any kind of radiological process can provide a clear diagnosis. The only thing we have at our disposal right now is the MMSE score.'

'This infantile test, you mean?'

'If you like . . .'

Infantile was the right word. I had to answer a few silly questions, say what the date was, which season it was, which country we lived in and which town. Then I had to remember a few idiotic words: *tree*, *carrot* and *lamp*. She formulated a far from elegant sentence, asked me to repeat it, then had me spell the word *world* backwards. One of the tasks was written on a sheet of paper, namely, 'Fold this piece of paper and slide it under one leg of your chair.' Really, some of the tests were so undemanding for a creature that prides itself on its one and a half kilos of cerebral sludge that I scarcely dared to answer all the questions incorrectly or fumble over the tasks. I needed to be careful not to betray myself by aiming for a disproportionately low score. It was only when I reached the last task, copying a picture of two interlinked pentagons, that I found something genuinely difficult.

My final score was 17 out of 30.

'See! He's passed!'

My wife, in a tone that had long been part of the aural furniture at home, along with the buzz of the fridge.

'Well, you can't really say he's passed . . . It's like this, Mrs De Petter: it's true that 17 out of 30 is more than fifty per cent. Just. But unfortunately for your husband this isn't a university entrance exam and this score actually means that his intellectual capacities are already severely diminished. In fact I can do little more than recommend that he be admitted to a specialised care facility. And as quickly as possible.'

I gave the doctor a friendly smile and hoped that my eyes were twinkling. Maybe she'd get an inkling of how happy her diagnosis had made me.

'But, doctor, that's impossible. You've made some kind of blunder. My husband was a librarian. He used to keep up his Latin by giving speeches to the sparrows in the garden. He wrote his dissertation on Erasmus. Someone like that can't—'

'Mrs De Petter, please, this disease doesn't care whose brain it is. It makes no distinction between smart and stupid. Your husband needs help. You must realise that. He's confused, he's lost the thread of his own thoughts, he's actually incredibly lonely and afraid. That's going to cause frustration and sometime soon maybe even aggression. He could lash out at you . . . And if he does he won't hold back, you can rest assured of that . . .'

Oh, no! Oh, my!

The doctor continued, 'Of course I understand all too well that receiving a diagnosis like this is far from pleasant. But I am a little taken aback that it can come as any kind of surprise to you, given how far the disease has already progressed. But it's Mr Cordier who needs our support now. He can't look after himself anymore. So please, make an effort and put yourself in second place. He's the one we're here for!'

And she turned away and continued the conversation with my daughter.

A memorable moment. And Moniek's expression was unforgettable too, her aggrieved lower lip shooting down like a lead weight.

In the car it took a long while before someone said a word. And because silence has always confronted her with things she doesn't have the character to bear, Moniek was the first to pipe up.

'That cow's on a nice little earner!' she blurted from the back seat. 'How long were we in there altogether? Half an hour? Forty minutes? She dishes up a few blatantly ridiculous questions for your father, then says, "He's three bricks shy of a load, that'll be 135 euros, thank you very much, bye!" and we just have to nod and smile. I'm sorry, but if I'd known it was that easy, I wouldn't have spent my glory days doing the ironing – I'd have become a doctor instead.'

Ignoring her mother, Charlotte pretended to be concentrating on the first signs of the evening rush hour and then, after a while, asked, 'Father, are you all right?' Resting her hand on my knee for a moment while she spoke.

It would have been fair to say I was all right. Exceptionally well, in fact. Officially senile. And soon to be a pharmacist's dream, a Memantine gobbler.

'How did the exam go?' I asked. 'Did I pass?'

And that silence was back again, shorter but even less comfortable than the last time.

'You passed,' Charlotte said. Her eyes were damp.

'What did I get?'

'A distinction!'

'Really?'

'Really.'

'Well, then it's my treat. Come on, where shall we eat?'

Brasserie Vivaldi is a good place to celebrate a dementia diagnosis, even if claims like that are generally easier to make than explain.

When, after a difficult drive, Charlotte finally pulled up in that establishment's car park, I crowed, 'Huh? Are we eating out? What a brilliant idea!' As happy as a child.

We sat down at a table next to the aquarium, which contained a sunken ship to remind the fish of their distant origins and a treasure chest with air bubbling up out of it.

Moniek's expression seemed to say, *What kind of non-sense is this, wasting money on a restaurant when somebody's just had half a death sentence?* And Charlotte, inspired by Dr Vancleemput's rigorous approach, barked, 'Look, Mother, if you want to deprive Father of any more pleasures, you'd better do it now, because you're right, soon it'll be too late!'

A cosy family outing, in other words.

Would we care for an aperitif?

I suggested a small glass of champagne and my daughter agreed, whereas my statutory consort stuck to water. 'Water, please. A simple glass of water. Tap water will do.'

In just a few days I'd be in a home and she'd only have herself to make miserable. I had the impression she'd decided to get started straight away.

'Happy birthday, Mother!' I said raising the bubbly.

'Happy birthday, Mum!' Charlotte played along. 'And many more to come!'

And so say all of us.

As usual, Charlotte hadn't found anything to her taste on the menu and asked if the cook couldn't come up with something vegetarian, it didn't matter what. Whereupon her mother butted in, snarling in F major:

'Can't you act like everyone else just once in your

life? Eating a little bit of meat's not going to kill you!'

Charlotte must have been about sixteen when she ruined an ordinary family meal by announcing that she couldn't see anything particularly appetising about mass slaughter and logistically optimised torture. Back in those days we'd hardly even heard of vegetarianism. Yes, in my professional capacity I had learnt that the writers Shelley and Shaw were not fond of our species' carnivorous tendencies, but that was in the nineteenth century, when the *belles* and not quite so *belles lettres* were teeming with morbid nutcases, and it was also the only fact on the subject I was able to come up with. Sure, we'd seen a few naked protesters agitating against the use of fur, but we couldn't help but notice that none of those politically committed wenches had been hard done by in the breast department. From our perspective on the sofa, it didn't seem like they were making much of a sacrifice by publicly displaying their perfect female curves. But vegetarianism, no, that was something the film stars of the day hadn't yet embraced. At least not as far as we knew. We attributed our daughter's determination to her age, that helped us put it into some kind of perspective, but otherwise we, as concerned and uninformed parents, were at our wits' end. Both Moniek and I, traditionally educated in the belief that meat kept you healthy and strong, tried to ward off TB and other dangers by eating steak as often as we could afford it; and now we were saddled with a child who had voluntarily renounced the benefits of beef. If anything our Hugo was the opposite: he had to force himself to stick his fork into a vegetable. But Charlotte . . . Anorexia, some people insisted. The spoilt generation, others pontificated. A whim of fashion, according to those in the know. And meanwhile we felt inadequate and were terrified that anaemia and vitamin deficiencies would soon have Charlotte shuffling from one hospital bed to the next.

It is one of my absolute lows as a father, and I fear Charlotte will never forget this particular scene, but it was around this time that I had the nerve to try to force her to eat a piece of meat – turkey breast – boldly asserting that I'd rather drop dead on the spot than tolerate her ruining her health with her adolescent rebellion.

She didn't touch the turkey and I didn't drop dead. Charlotte had won the battle and accepted the song and dance she got from then on every time we were invited somewhere to eat. She resigned herself to making do with a cheese croquette while the others couldn't stop going on about how tender the duck was. Helpless cooks thought they were offering her an alternative by serving up half a bucket of iceberg lettuce. She patiently bore questions like 'Are you allowed to eat fish?' or 'Are mussels animals too?' and saw herself banned from numerous back gardens once barbecue season arrived and mankind was falsely united around a couple of kilos of sausages.

Many conflicts later we were in Brasserie Vivaldi and Moniek still hadn't reconciled herself to the convictions of her long-grown-up daughter. 'Just take the chicken, I've heard it tastes just like that Quorn of yours! Your metabolism will be so overjoyed it'll be doing somersaults inside your body!'

But the waiter was able offer her a moussaka made with a meat substitute and that really was vastly superior to the eternal cheese croquette.

'I'm not such a difficult character,' Moniek told the young man. 'The meatballs in tomato sauce will be just fine. Simple meatballs in simple tomato sauce.'

And since I was no longer considered especially independent, she ordered for me too while she was at it: my personal classic, steak with pepper sauce, rare, and chips with extra salt.

'No,' I corrected her. 'No, I'll have the vegetarian moussaka too.'

'OK, fine, two vegetarian moussakas. Got it. Anything else?'

'Um, maybe another glass of champagne? Yes, I see my daughter nodding . . . Two glasses of champagne! And some more tap water for my wife. Thank you.'

★

If I had still wanted to die in my own house, speed would have been of the essence, because it had finally arrived: the long-awaited day I would take up residence in an old folks' home – Winterlight, as I'd discover a few hours later. A run-of-the-mill Saturday, created for cleaning windows, washing cars, doing the shopping, ferrying children to sports' clubs and taking rubbish to the dump. But not for me.

Our Hugo had long stopped seeing his father's birthday as an obligation to honour the parental home with his presence. Pumped-up commercial celebrations like New Year, Mother's Day and Christmas left him cold, and I actually envied him that enormously. He was a completely unsentimental character with a busy life that left little room for cake and chats with his makers.

77

Moniek dedicated melodramatic arias to the subject, accusing her son of ingratitude, which only reduced his desire to come back next time.

Now he was here. Badly shaven. But here.

Perhaps his mother – or his sister – had appealed to his masculine expertise and the attendant responsibilities. And though he was no longer a young Spartacus but a desperate forty-something in search of the right pillow to finally vanquish his neck ache, Hugo could still be of service to the family by disassembling a small wardrobe and putting it back together somewhere else. There was also an old television cabinet to get down from the attic and the single bed in the guest room that would be making the move with me: men's work!

It was a mystery to me who'd come up with the idea, but they had evidently decided that my last breakfast at home would be a family event with all of us. The children, Moniek and me. Without any annoying in-laws. Just the four of us.

Charlotte arrived on the scene with her eyes still showing signs of a crying fit. And with a bag full of pastries, fresh from the bakery and still slightly warm. Everyone in the family knew my weakness for vanilla cream. Before taking his place in the electric chair, serial killer Ted Bundy requested steak and eggs; Victor Feguer ('the last man Uncle Sam executed') swore by an unpitted olive; I definitely had no objections to a

Berliner as my last meal. Filled with pastry cream (I didn't like the jam variety). That's just to show how delicious I found them. But when I was in my prime Moniek had deprived me of this treat as much as she possibly could: 'Aren't you fat enough? Your arteries are already clogged up from all that wine you guzzle!'

This time she kept her trap shut.

Were my suspicions correct and had she taken some kind of sedative?

Hugo squeezed oranges and, judging by the adroitness with which he squirted juice at the ceiling, this was the first time in his existence. Giuseppe Tartini's cello concerto was playing, a composition I hadn't expected to hear again until my own funeral. My wife didn't like it; she didn't like Tartini at all. Just as she didn't like Bach or Pärt or Bruch. My taste was too melancholy for her. Definitely so at breakfast. 'Coffee and a funeral march, what a way to start the day!'

And I took it and never even had the balls to get myself some headphones. I took it and, with all my stuffy, fuddy-duddy ways, derided headphones as *the* symbol of a new, antisocial generation. How much more I could have enjoyed music . . .

But now, in a hopeless, despairing, futile attempt to make amends, I was being mollycoddled.

Once again Charlotte turned out to be the mainstay of this broken family.

79

'Father . . .'

'Yes?'

'Father, do you know what's happening today?'

'Yes.'

'What?'

I didn't say anything.

'What, Father? Can you tell me? What are we going to do today?'

'Yes.'

'We're going to take you to a home!'

This conversation was too much for Moniek, who had started on the washing up.

'It's only temporary, Father. I want you to know that it's only temporary and that we're doing it because we love you and want to take care of you as best we can.'

'Yes.'

'But you've just been through a very turbulent period and you need to recover a little in your head. Once the tests have been done and you're back on track, you'll be coming straight back home. Do you understand?'

'Yes.'

The ease with which she lied to me was impressive. All with the kindest of intentions, perhaps, but I couldn't help wondering how often she'd gulled me before. What a talent for dissemblance! Admittedly, I wasn't well placed to reproach her on that account.

°○°

We were going to drive there in two vehicles. Apprehensive as he was about overwrought emotions and the extremely predictable blubbering of the females once I was being driven out of our front gate never to return, Hugo had decided to fill his car with all the necessary gear: three suitcases full of clothes – pyjamas and tracksuit bottoms mainly – plus the furniture for my new room. Moniek and I could go in Charlotte's car.

'It's all packed,' Hugo panted.

A death knell would have sounded more cheerful.

There was nothing keeping me here.

The neighbours had positioned themselves strategically to watch my silent departure. One was weeding his front garden, another was pushing a lawnmower over the same patch of lawn for the fourth time that morning. Many of them were contemporaries, of course, who had moved to the street at more or less the same time as us. Our houses are more or less the same age. Our bodies too. Our children grew up with each other, we received our first summons for a prostate check together and talked about it at the same street parties. Perhaps somewhere, in a back room of the heart, they were saddened for my sake alone, but mainly they experienced my moving to a home as a confrontation with themselves: *their* generation, *their* imminent demise.

Marie-Louise from number 31 was the only one to

stand out on the street unabashed with a good half of her face buried in a hankie. She too was made up of sixty per cent water and that morning it was bursting to get out. From the top end, of course.

'Dad, will you come and sit next to me in the car? With Mother in the back? Hugo will follow in his own car . . . Come on!'

Although she was already having the greatest difficulty keeping a grip on herself, I looked my daughter in the eye and said,

'You don't think I'm going to fall for that, do you?'

'What do you mean, Father?'

'What do I mean? That I'm smarter than you think, that's what I mean!'

'Just tell me. What's wrong?'

'Take a look at the car, Charlotte! What do you see?'

'I don't see anything.'

'You don't see anything, you say. Look closer!'

'I don't see anything, Dad, really I don't. Come on, tell me. What am I supposed to see?'

'The caravan! It hasn't been hitched on yet. We almost set off without it again!'

His heart wasn't really in it, but in the end Hugo gave in to his sister's demands and hitched the caravan onto the car. Plus the towing mirrors – to avoid accidents!

And when, after many delays, we finally left, I said to Charlotte:

'Look at all the neighbours out gawking at us! They're green with envy. Go on, give 'em a toot.'

And, encouraged by that mischievous honking, I wound down my window and waved wildly all the way down Azalea Street. Whereupon someone, three guesses who (first name rhymes with 'pique', surname with 'fetter'), said:

'He may be soft in the head but at least he's not suffering.'

★

I'm crossing the Styx and taking: a tube of toothpaste (just for a joke), a stray Joseph Roth quote,
the wondrous memory of an ardent kiss I never got,
bread crumbs, greater solace than a good Berliner ever
offered me, a stanza of 'Auntie Bonanza', the longing
for a T-shirt emblazoned with the words LIFE BEGINS
AT SEVENTY-FOUR . . .

★

So, this is it then, my hard-won terminus: a tiny room
four metres by five – something like that, obviously
I haven't measured it. At first I was offended by the
shabby furniture Moniek had filled it with. She simply

84

couldn't forgive me for forgetting her, so much so that it was now futile for me to search my mental catacombs for her name. Worse still: according to my seemingly ailing brain, this lady who claimed to be married to me had never even existed. And for that she was making me suffer with a cheap mattress and a tiny, obsolete TV.

My wardrobe: a dilapidated, wobbling monster that had only found a buyer in the form of my wife after a month-long expedition from flea market to flea market. I had forfeited the right to quality and it was obviously no longer worth investing in my comfort.

'Why put money into a new, solid wardrobe? It's not as if he'd even notice the difference!'

The beauty of an austere interior was something Moniek had never grasped, which explained why she had felt the compulsion to fill every square millimetre in Azalea Street with vases, peacock feathers, clocks and suchlike. This time she demonstrated her fear of empty spaces by cramming as many picture frames as humanly possible into my small and already claustrophobic room. And in those frames: pictures of herself! Moniek with her husband. Moniek with her children. Moniek with her husband *and* her children. Moniek solo. And not a single spontaneous snap in the whole collection. The ice queen of the pose preferred her portraits in a setting of flowers or shrubs. She also had the peculiar tic of needing to *touch* those flowers or shrubs for the camera.

It resulted in highly ridiculous photos: a woman with a smile picked up from a toothpaste advertisement, standing there as stiff as a plank and staring into the lens while simultaneously palpating a hydrangea.

Photo sessions with Moniek were a torment for the whole family. She ordered everyone around, telling them where and how to stand. And she's definitely not one for practical jokes. When the kids were still little and enjoyed poking their tongues out or playfully crossing their eyes at the camera, their mother saw it as a vulgar assault on her personal well-being.

'Is this how you want to go down in history? As a cross-eyed otter? Come on, tuck in that shirt and stop looking like a freak! One, two, three and smiley smiles!'

That was her slogan: 'Smiley smiles.'

Everyone always had to grab hold of each other too, during those supposed immortalisations of hers. The few times she laid an arm around my shoulders was for the camera. The assigned photographer had to accept her commands too. Whether or not to use the flash, which angle, which clouds and pine trees to include in the shot, if and where exactly our legs should be cut off: she decided everything and woe betide anyone who dared to flout her instructions. And as if magnesium was still being used to reduce the exposure time, as if it wasn't just an ordinary family member standing there with an ordinary camera but Diego Velázquez with a freshly stretched canvas, she decreed that all present remain motionless until the image had been captured. 'Hold your breath, don't move!'

Digital photography was one advance too many as far as I was concerned. Because from that moment on Moniek could immediately check the results of each photo shoot. And discover that they needed to be improved upon. The candles on my antepenultimate birthday cake, for instance, had to be blown out and relit no less than nine times, by me, before she gave her imprimatur to the photographic record of that hardly historic occasion.

So obviously I was far from happy with all that staged family bliss hanging in my room. One of the first times Moniek came to visit me she discovered that I had removed all, and I mean *all,* of the photos from their frames and replaced them with pictures and advertisements torn out of old magazines. Where previously my wife had stood below the Eiffel Tower with a handbag clamped under one arm, there was now a photo of a discount prosciutto, just €19.99 a kilo. I replaced the portraits of our grandchildren – correction, the portraits of Moniek with our grandchildren – with newspaper photos of car crashes, and our wedding photo made way for an aerial shot of a South American slum. The head nurse had to console her, insisting that no matter how you looked at it, you couldn't say her husband was comparing her to a leg of ham. Not exactly. It was in the nature of my disease to manifest itself as a series of unpredictable fancies. There was no reasoning behind my actions, they were the empty deeds of a man who has lost the blueprints to his own soul.

The head nurse had put it beautifully. Bravo.

Even more disgraceful than all those lying photos were the religious symbols Moniek had catapulted into my existence *in extremis*. A crucifix over *my* bed, just imagine! 'It can't do any harm!' she said. And on my old-fashioned bedside cabinet she planted a monstrous statue – bisque, I think – of Rita of Cascia, patron saint of hopeless cases. Maybe Moniek was guilty of stupidity rather than malice and simply suffered from a conviction that idolatry was part and parcel of being in a home. But a person – and I'm talking about myself here – who grew up in a society in which religion went unquestioned and considers his agnosticism an achievement, the product of deep and courageous thought, can only feel ridiculed by having the label 'Catholic' stuck to his forehead. I felt philosophically swindled by my lawfully wedded wife and regretted not being able to step out of character for a minute to point this gruesome misrepresentation out to Winterlight's nursing staff. It annoyed me immensely, being henceforth noted down on death's waiting list as a believer. The first rattle in my throat or tiniest bit of coughed-up blood will have a priest scurrying to my bedside with a breviary and an aspergillum. I feel like crawling away in shame at the thought of almost certainly having a church funeral.

Fortunately many years ago, and without Moniek's knowledge, I had stated in my will that I didn't give two hoots what they did with my bodily remains – as long as they didn't stuff me in the ground next to my wife! Moniek and I had spent more than enough nights lying next to each other like corpses, we didn't need to do it again in a family plot. Let her lie in her tomb alone! She'll be nice and comfortable. Under her marble, her cross, her photo with her toothpaste-ad smile and the pot of flowers she won't be able to touch for the photo nobody will take.

I don't wish to laud myself as some kind of iconoclast, but I did smash the statue of St Rita to pieces. The patron saint of lost causes was swept into a dustpan and ingloriously tipped on top of the household rubbish, nappies and used needles.

I had even more fun getting rid of that half-naked Christ. Late at night I would weep terribly – an anxiety attack was overdue anyway, as were the hallucinations.

Tarzan was in my room and was going to kill me. Help! Help!

Curvy Cora began by reassuring me. She didn't want to ridicule my fears, but she couldn't see Tarzan anywhere. Maybe he'd already left, that was possible, because she couldn't see him under the bed either. And she hushed me to sleep with a sweetie under my tongue that worked like a dream.

But of course Tarzan kept coming to visit. Night after night after night. And why not? After all, Indians with tomahawks had plagued my grandmother.

'There! Tarzan! Over my pillow! On the wall! Heeeelp!'

'That's not Tarzan, Désiré. That's Jesus!'

That only made my panic attack even more feverish.

They couldn't keep slipping me knockout drops and injecting me full of tranquillisers. Or tying me down – a disgraceful practice that, to my immense surprise, is still quite accepted and hurt my wrists and ankles like hell. So the easiest solution turned out to be the cheapest and best: the crucifix was simply removed from my room.

And believe it or not, Tarzan never came back.

A radio, yes, I got to bring one of those too. When they plugged it in to test it, a criminologist was speaking. He insisted that our capital was much less dangerous than public opinion would have us believe. Yes, yes, the odd lamentable death did occur here and there in the filthy alleyways. And yes, modest civil wars were stirred up by text message after football matches. And, yes again, both bus drivers and pensioners were sometimes attacked for less than the contents of a handbag. But people who were desperate to be murdered were wasting their time hanging round the city's depressing metro stations. No, if a horrific crime was what you were after, you were still better off tying the knot. Statistics proved that the chance of being married to your own murderer was much, much higher than the likelihood of encountering him as a stranger on the streets of the metropolis. Marriage was still our most dangerous form of criminal organisation by far, and you never heard any extremist parties raging against *that* ancient bourgeois institution. They even had the gall to talk about the family as the cornerstone of society!

'Fine, that seems to be working,' Moniek mumbled, silencing the criminologist with a single finger on the power switch.

'Don't turn it off,' I said, waking with a start. 'He was just making a very interesting point.'

A lucid phase, you see. I needed them sometimes too.

I watch TV, albeit with the greatest reluctance. I do it to avoid giving myself away. Because dementia sufferers are expected to be tireless when it comes to sitting in front of the idiot box. Abetted by the emptiness of most of the programmes, I train the glassiest eyes I can muster at the merry pleasure-vendors on the screen and stare at them indolently until I can't help but fall asleep and the nurses come to take me back to bed.

Radio is a better companion for someone who is holding death at bay a little longer but has otherwise sabotaged all his bridges to life. Classical music mainly, but without going into the composers or entertaining myself with post-mortem discussions about interpretations, variations or whatever. Listening only for the sake of the music, as if it exists by itself and doesn't need to be made by a human being. Fabulous. And then it's funny when a nurse wants to do me a favour. She sees me drowsing in my armchair and takes pity on me for suffering the scourge of a cello sonatina when I'm so incapacitated by clumsiness, I can't change the station by myself. So, without waiting to ask, she waltzes up to the radio and splashes off through the airwaves in search of sounds for the crowd. Tra-la-la and oompahpah.

'There you go, Désiré, this music will cheer you up a little, I'm sure . . .'

She means well, no doubt about that.

Recently my most faithful companion has been, somewhat surprisingly, a dog, Pablo by name, even though many of the residents address him with the name of the dog that played a role in their own past and has been buried for decades in the vegetable garden of a residence that will soon be divvied up between relatives who are united only by their mutual loathing.

Small and hairy, Pablo is happy to sit on any lap at all and provides many of the oldies with the pleasure of still being able to express their love for someone or something. Neither fine hand control nor the power of speech is required and he undoubtedly produces little judders of joy in the hearts of those who stroke him. A panting antidepressant on four foreshortened legs. I had heard that more and more institutions were successfully deploying pets as staff members. The price of a bag of dog biscuits pales into insignificance compared even to the meagre wages of a care worker. And you can rightly ask yourself, what does a dying person the most good: the satisfied silence of a hedonist on their lap or the much too noisy chatter of a bum washer whose morale has been eroded by the low pay?

I never had a dog, although my children whined enough about getting one when they were little and I had secretly hoped it was a battle they would win. Unfortunately Moniek wasn't fond of animals. She snipped live spiders in half with scissors or sucked them up the vacuum-cleaner hose. That's how much they scared her. Dogs were even worse, immune as they were to scissors and hoovers.

'A dog? They have fangs: they bite! Plus they track all kinds of filth and disease into the house. No, thanks.'

It's fabulous now to have Moniek come to visit just when Pablo is sitting on my knee. To hear her bray, 'Désiré, please, put that animal down. It's getting its disgusting germs all over your clothes!'

'Who are you?' I always ask at moments like that. 'You won't find anything here, it's all safe in the bank. Get out of here quick smart or I'll call the police and set my dog on you.'

If she ignores my warning or laughs it off, I can always scream the house down, using the screech of panic I have now almost perfected. These are the moments when I crow with pleasure on the inside and know that my adventure has been worth all the trouble.

Smiley smile.

★

I had almost given up on the possibility of ever seeing her again when suddenly there she was: Rosa Rozendaal! In the dining room! Toothless and wrapped in a beige dressing gown. Sucking her thumb, as if she found it necessary to emphasise that she was in her second childhood. If I hadn't known better, I would have sworn that only an incorrigible optimist could believe that this vacant head had once belonged to such a stunning woman. Whose beauty was preserved now only in the dreams of those who couldn't have her. I studied this stranded wreck's appearance closely, as nothing could be more likely than a case of mistaken identity, but I wasn't mistaken: it was Rosa and Rosa alone, parked in her wheelchair in a corner of the dining room. Rosa and no one else, and I still don't know how I conjured up the self-control to restrain myself and not immediately burst out of my skin with joy.

It had been months and months since I'd heard that she

was suffering from arteriosclerosis and had been admitted to a home so that her circle of acquaintance could get used to the idea of soon forgetting her completely. The chances of her having died in the meantime had been more than significant. But look. There she was. Rosa.

I've been able to observe the aging process in my own antique mug slowly, one day at a time. Of course, what I see when I stand in front of the mirror to shave is more a shrivelled apple than a face, and I don't find anything flattering about it at all. But I've never been outraged by the sight of myself as a decrepit old gent. As far as I know, I always wear my present-day face in my dreams, my *visage du jour*, and in my nightmares too I am always the age I was when I went to bed. Being young and myself once again, re-experiencing even a few minutes of my youth, is a privilege that even the magical-realist scriptwriter of my dreams won't grant me. The appearance of the man on the other side of the washbasin has progressed through time together with my thoughts; my face is the perfect expression of how I think and feel.

In a nutshell: I'm at peace with my ugliness.

When I summon up an image of my grandmother, I generally see her as a woman of around sixty. Which means that I now think of my grandmother as someone who is significantly younger than me.

Rosa Rozendaal's appearance had been frozen in my memory the way she looked when we were standing together in the car park of the Albatross Party Centre, just before my bungling banished her from my future. A girl, almost a woman, in the warm but much too short springtime of her life, with the hairdo that happened to be all the rage back then.

Long before computer programs that could accurately anticipate the aging of a face had been designed (with the aim of tracking down people who had been missing for decades), I, as a young monkey, enjoyed fantasising about how my friends would look once they were grandads: who would be bald, who would be grey, who would be crippled and who would be sprightly. I imagined them with moustaches, hunches and gummy mouths. But I never touched my image of Rosa. It would have been sacrilege.

Instead of my imagination, time had gone to work.

And that's why I declare war on the callow romantic who claimed that beauty's ruins were more beautiful than beauty itself. Because war is what he deserves. War, or at least a better pair of glasses. Because there was no way the impact of this withered old woman's appearance could bear comparison to the uproar she caused in the hearts of every healthy young man who laid eyes on her more than half a century ago.

°o°

Was she looking at me, or was it my imagination?

Rosa. Rosa pimpinellifolia. Rosa majalis. Rosa rubiginosa. Rosa tomentella.

Along with my euphoria at this reunion, I was also seized by a degree of despondency. Personally I wasn't bothered by the setting in which I would spend the rest of my life. On the contrary, the surrounding misery was part of the game. But seeing Rosa live out her days in this place, in such a state of neglect, saddened me. If she could take a few firm steps back in time, Rosa would quickly aim her car straight at an oak to avoid this dismal end.

At the very least I would have expected her to have been admitted to a more luxurious nursing home. Though on the other hand, if you consider the price they already charged for an institution as dilapidated as this: an average monthly wage, not counting doctor's bills, medicine and nappies. And you still have to give your laundry to your kids. And what you get for that hard-earned cash is a fair chance of lying on the cold floor for three hours if you happen to tumble out of bed, simply because there aren't enough staff to regularly stick their noses into every room. Take my neighbour, for example, who recently spent an entire night lying naked on the floor, whimpering all the while, and had to wait until the sun was up and the first trolley with nursing supplies was thundering down the corridor. It's a pathetic thing, listening to the bleating of someone who hardly has the strength to move his vocal chords.

I know that Liesbeth in room 16 has oral cancer. She has to rinse her mouth three times a day but that's often simply forgotten and not just by her. Her rinsing cup fills up with threads of pus and little bits of flesh that fall off the insides of her cheeks and they don't get round to replacing it until a full day later, if then. The difficulties she has chewing are not always communicated clearly to the kitchen either, so sometimes on a Sunday they might serve her a gristly steak and even make a big song and dance about it. 'Look what I've got for you today, Liesbeth, a delicious steak! If you listen closely you'll hear it moo, that's how fresh it is! A Sunday treat! Enjoy . . .' And Liesbeth, the sheep, is much too well behaved and full of blind respect for a home that still, tenuously, falls under the auspices of an order of nuns. She keeps her trap shut and leaves the steak untouched on her plate. And who can blame her? Maybe starvation is a gentler death than cancer.

As soon as Rosa appeared on the scene I gave up the hard-won peace of my room and willingly let the staff drag me out to all kinds of moronic activities. The manager of the home explained this behavioural watershed to my wife with the words:

'Your husband has adapted wonderfully well to what is for him a new, strange and often frightening environment. After being admitted, many of our residents keep up the delusion that they will only be staying here for a few days at most, and then fall into a deep and persistent depression when it finally gets through to them that their ties to the home front have been severed forever . . .'

That explained me happily abandoning my radio in favour of an afternoon of bingo or, on a comparable level, snakes and ladders, in the hope of seeing Rosa there too. It was clear that I was venturing onto thin ice. Childish as these games are, they present numerous pitfalls for anyone who's only pretending to be gaga, and the chances of my being unmasked were too great for comfort. I wasn't even sure if approaching someone else was consistent with my syndrome. Dubious. If I spent too long looking at Rosa, keeping her in my sights as it were, and sat down next to her at the table whenever I had the chance, would I be undermining the plausibility of my dementia? No idea, but caution was called for.

What's that? Arts and crafts? Come and get me! I painted Christmas-tree decorations on command, Easter eggs and carnival masks, I made paper chains and blew up balloons, or at least demonstrated an intent to do so (making sure, of course, to get more spit than air in the balloon).

But most of all I looked forward to the singing session, which they called memory choir. An innovation in aged care. Because now that it's been scientifically proven that the songs of one's youth stand relatively firm in a leaking memory, so-called memory choirs have sprung up here and there in old folks' homes. Singing – that's all the Vienna Fogeys' Choir has to do. The ancient past, memories of fun songs, melodies from a bygone era. According to the specialists it does the old dears good to exercise their memories, and singing improves both their morale and their self-confidence. It would never have occurred to Nurse Dirk, our choir's conductor, that one of the residents might have been a member of a choir as a child. I mean a real choir, where you put your heart and soul into Bach cantatas. The repertoire of the memory choir was limited to golden oldies, popular crap, entertainment for the masses. Common denominators are seldom elevated. It wasn't the end of the world; I kept my cantatas to myself and yodelled along to the musical success stories of an earlier age. And realised, to my own astonishment, that all those lyrics had indeed been resistant to the erosion of time. Without my making the slightest attempt to remember them.

Rosa sometimes passed on the 'crafternoons' and bingo sessions, to her credit, but when the memory choir was assembled she was almost always there. If I managed to be allocated a chair next to hers, I was the happiest man in the world and surrounding galaxies, and sang along with an enthusiasm I hadn't thought possible:

*I might not remember your name, but I'll never forget*
   *your sweet kiss,*
*Your love was to me just a game, but now in my*
   *dreams it is bliss,*
*I never met another girl who meant so much to me,*
*I said goodbye and led a life of lonesome misery.*

Every now and then Rosa and I looked at each other while warbling Ray Franky's tired old hit and I couldn't help but notice that she was no longer a shrivelled vegetable in a wheelchair: she was a happy woman. During those magical moments a big grin appeared in the mass of grey skin that made up her face. Her yesterday had gone away, but she was happy as long as that one song lasted.

*Though I never did taste her sweet kiss, I'll always*
   *remember her name.*
*When she comes to my dreams it is bliss, the love that*
   *I felt was no game.*

Someone else who was and still is a devotee of the ideology of group singing is, of course, Camp Commandant Alzheimer. You can tell that he feels cheated by his own capitulating legs, because he'd much rather be wearing boots than those shabby slippers, and instead of sitting in a wheelchair, he wishes he was singing his songs marching. But even so he blossoms completely and puts some vibrato into his flaccid vocal cords when he joins the memory choir. Once he gets going there's no stopping him and all by himself he rattles off his whole, rather unusual oeuvre:

*Sharpen up the long knives on the pavement stones,*
*Plunge the knives in deep and make the Jew blood flow,*
*Blood must flow, coming fast and thick,*
*And we shit upon the freedom,*
*Of this Jewish republic.*

As I said, a very happy man, and living proof that a memory choir like this really is a highly economical way of easing the suffering of the elderly.

They always concluded the choral sessions with a few dirty songs. It's no secret that old men and women have one-track minds and a passionate interest in the contents of underpants. The more respectable the position they held in their heyday, the greater their love for the racier chanson. Ex-teachers, missionaries who have returned from a malarial zone, newsreaders, justices of the peace, former government ministers, the fathers of large and devout families: they're all crazy about the smut they once avoided in public. But time knows no pity, King Hourglass comes for us in the end and, when he does, nature reclaims everything culture tried to suppress for all those years.

A perennial hit in Winterlight Geriatric is the famous 'Ballad of Auntie Bonanza', which was sung in the streets of our youth by drunk labourers and picked up by adolescent reprobates:

*Oh, she's as blind as a mole with a stinky old hole, it's yer Auntie Bonanza . . .*

This song always aroused great enthusiasm in Rosa too, who sang along with the following seven lines without a single mistake, as if she'd been rehearsing on the sly in her room.

It's a shame we don't get to do performances with this strange choir of ours. How I would have loved to see Moniek De Petter in the audience!

The exercise classes under the supervision of an accordionist and a geriatric physiotherapist never won me over. It was a missed opportunity to see Rosa Rozendaal, but it was too difficult for me to get my musculoskeletal system moving again. Nobody grows more supple with the years and I'd never been what you'd call loose-limbed anyway.

Until recently my day was Friday, dance day. That was when Lorenzo – Frank Sinatra to the power of minus ten – came to plink out evergreens and smoochers on his synthesizer. Although he was never really in tune, the thin moustache he'd cultivated to conceal at least part of his baby face made him incredibly popular with the great-grannies. I wouldn't be surprised if he wasn't sometimes left an entire estate by a widow whose only joy in life was provided by Lorenzo, the pancake-house pianist.

Someone in my condition can't display much get-up-and-go, so I had to await my fate apathetically and dance with whichever partner the staff, with a pretence of cheerfulness, allocated me. Which mostly meant shuffling around while leaning on a nurse. Strangers in the night. But one day I would be hitched to Rosa and if the pharmaceuticals were able to give her the strength to leave her wheelchair for five minutes then . . . then I would take her in my arms and dance with her. A jive in a thousand slow-motion beats. And when I had assured myself that none of the alert souls around us were listening in, I would whisper in her ear:

'Rosa, it's me, Désiré Cordier. How would you like it if we stepped outside for a moment, to get a breath of fresh air, it's much too hot in here anyway . . .'

*

Between the ages of sixteen and thirty I was a regular theatre-goer and interpreted everything that happened on stage as an abstraction of real life. Nowadays I try to amuse myself by seeing scenes from real life as theatre. Sometimes that's useful. Like when I was sitting in the garden of the home waiting for the bus that never came. The sun was shining, directing its bright malice at the nation's students who had to spend the rest of the season studying for their exams. The windows of almost every room in the home were open, and through one of them a fascinating radio play reached me. A powerful voice, suitable for open-air operas and election speeches:

'So that's how you do it, is it? Ramming nutrients into the veins of an old man who doesn't want to eat!'

Unfortunately I couldn't hear the nurse's answer, but it was easy to guess from the tirade that followed.

'Of course my father's not eating. And why not, do you think? Has he got a problem with his gullet? No. Have his jaws frozen up? No. So, nurse, what could it be? Shall I tell you? Oh, wait, I've already told you, my father's not eating because he doesn't want to eat! He does not want to! And why does my father not want to eat? Because he's more or less had it with this life! Because he wants to die, if you understand that better! That's why. It beggars belief that you seem to be incapable of seeing something so simple. You must be as blind as a bat. As blind as a bat or as thick as a brick. And what do you lot do when someone here doesn't want to stick the food in their mouth anymore? You inject the whole meal into their arm: starter, soup, main course and pudding, the whole *plat du jour*, right into the bloodstream! Enjoy your meal, grandad. Just look at the poor guy's skinny little arms. They're purple from all the needles you've poked into them. You must be a monster to be capable of something like this. And if my father tears the needles out of his arm, which he has every right to do, you restrain him as if he's a criminal. Even worse, because here in this country you have to do something bloody atrocious before they deprive you of your liberty and tie you up . . . May I ask what you're going to do when my father doesn't have any arms left? When you've buggered up every last vein with your catheters? Are you going to start pumping his meals up his arse or what . . . ?'

A beautiful scene, presented with gusto, but, alas, I missed out on the climax thanks to the sudden closure of that particular window.

During this moving performance, I was sharing the bus shelter in the garden with a small, scrawny man I guessed to be in his mid-eighties. I knew him by sight from the corridors and dining room. Sometimes he participated in a snakes-and-ladders afternoon, if you could call it participating; he never did much more than wobble back and forth with his upper body while they wiped the drool off his chin. He wore Jesus sandals and had enormous holes in his socks that his big toes stuck out of. The only thing he could still do properly in this life was roll cigarettes and then smoke them. One after the other.

He coughed.

I looked at him and asked, 'When's the 77 due? I have to get to my piano lesson on time.'

'Seven past the hour and thirty-four past the hour!' And he spat a tobacco-juice-coloured gob onto the ground.

That seemed an excellent conclusion to our conversation, without a doubt the most fascinating I'd had with a fellow resident since my arrival at Winterlight. He, however, felt differently, and took me by surprise with a disconcerting observation:

'You're making a mess of it. I'd take a bit more care if I was you, cos one of these days you're going to get caught.'

There are nutcases all over the place, especially round here.

'Pardon?' I said, not entirely at ease.

'It's obvious you're faking it. You exaggerate.'

'What do you mean?'

'You know what I mean. You're guilty of over-acting. A real ham. There aren't any bats in your belfry, no matter how hard you pretend otherwise.'

'Wow! So that means you're . . .'

Incredible. I was completely bowled over. Unmasked by a dishevelled, grimy old man.

I said, 'That was you, wasn't it, last week? Who suddenly showed up at the breakfast table in the nude, crying because Mummy hadn't come to pick you up from school.'

'You have to go that extra mile.'

'I'm impressed. I don't think I could manage that – not yet. Wandering the corridors in my birthday suit, no, I'm not ready for that.'

'Sooner or later you'll have to. It's an important phase . . . Do you already shit the bed?'

'Not every night. Three or four times a week. It's disgusting. But I've peed on the mat!'

'And your wife?'

'I don't recognise her anymore.'

'And your children?'

'My children? Complete strangers who come to pick up my dirty clothes every Saturday.'

'Excellent. Very good.'

And here was me thinking I'd left the folly of human interaction behind. A man (a husband and father, a dedicated employee, an honest taxpayer, respectable, nothing to hide) thinks he's the world's most adventurous old-age pensioner, the only one crazy enough to act on an impulse to pretend he's suffering from dementia. His plan succeeds – he even manages to convince the doctors of the neurofibrillary mess inside his skull – and he arrives triumphant and with renewed self-respect in a specialised institution, only to be forced to conclude that he is ab-so-lute-ly un-original. Holy shit!

I was immediately gripped by the fantasy that it might not be limited to just two Thespian greybeards, that I could be surrounded by more bright sparks than I thought!

And the surprising windfall; the possibility Rosa Rozendaal might be all there too! Definitely, she must be. When I thought of the look she gave me at memory choir . . .

'Do you think we're the only con artists here?' I asked my unexpected comrade-in-arms. 'Are there any others?'

Because if he'd managed to catch me out, it seemed only logical that he would have a good impression of the authenticity of the other dementia patients in the building. But he only shrugged.

'Take that milksop in room 18, the poor guy who sits there cutting those stupid pictures out of *Miaow!* when his wife comes to visit with her lover? Is he faking it?'

Again he shrugged.

'And that former camp guard?' I persisted. 'Walter De Bodt. Camp Commandant Alzheimer, I call him.'

'Hard to say.'

'He's at least got a good reason for acting like his attic's been vacated. Don't you reckon?'

'I told you, I don't know. But if that war criminal is a malingerer, his acting's a lot better than yours.'

And he rolled himself another cigarette.

I realised my inquisitiveness might annoy him, but took the risk of asking the one, obvious question:

'You're free not to answer, of course, but now I'm very curious as to what led you to feign dementia . . .'

'Mediocrity, I guess.'

'Mediocrity?'

'Being like everyone else and finally having enough of it.'

'Explain.'

'The five most common self-recriminations of the dying are: one, they worked too much. Two, they lived their lives according to the expectations of others. Three, they lost touch with their friends. Four, they didn't make themselves happy enough. And five, they didn't express their feelings enough . . . That fifth and final point doesn't bother me too much personally, but the other four more or less match the main themes of my life. Number two the most . . .'

'I understand.'

'And also,' he continued, 'I needed to be alone with myself again. Outside this home there's a world where all you do is talk. Talk, talk, talk and then talk some more. And listen, or at least pretend to listen, to people who talk, talk, talk. And hear them talking over each other, talking, talking. You have family and other obligations, and often that comes down to talking and listening, and I just didn't feel like it anymore – the whole social rigmarole. I wanted to finally have some peace and quiet to be alone with my thoughts. Here I can do that, more or less. It's the only place that accepts me being completely introverted. It was my last chance. And you? What gave you the idea?'

I wasn't entirely sure I could adequately explain my philosophy to a complete stranger off the top of my head like that, so I asked for a cigarette to gain some time. I hadn't smoked since I was twenty-one. Before then I'd always enjoyed it: I liked the taste and, as a permanently insecure youth, I'd been gratified that something as pathetic as a cigarette immediately gave me a pose to adopt. But times and customs have changed and so has our view of tobacco. And I had a girlfriend who took charge of her future family's life and demanded that I give up that stinking habit. Well, it *was* unhealthy and it did make you die young. Even if my chain-smoking buddy in the bus shelter wasn't providing definitive proof of the latter. Truth be told, after more than half a century, I stuck a fag between my lips and it was as if I'd smoked the last one just an hour ago, that's how familiar it felt. I didn't cough and only felt a slight, yet far from unpleasant dizziness. A most delicious experience, one that did me good after weeks of living off the meals produced in Winterlight Geriatric's low-fat, low-salt soup kitchen.

°₀°

'So, *do* you know why you spend your days wandering around here in your pyjamas?'

Yes, I knew why.

'*Life seemed to go faster than thoughts,*' I declaimed much too solemnly. '*And before he had made a decision, he was an old man . . .*'

They weren't my words, I had plucked them from the mouth of a character in a novel.

'You see,' I said, quickly trying to justify my – admittedly ridiculous – affectation, 'I was a librarian. A very contented librarian. I've always relied on books and I never minded supporting my own thoughts with the thoughts of others. So that quote means something to me.'

'That's the most important thing,' he answered drily, 'its meaning something to *you*.'

He was probably already regretting striking up a conversation with me. I could tell. Despite sharing a fate, we would never have become friends in real life – not when it still resembled a life.

Besides gobbledegook, I hadn't said anything at all for months. Now I was in an unforeseen conversation and found it, to my astonishment, exhausting. Soon this lack of linguistic fitness would come in handy when I embarked on the aphasic and, as far as I was concerned, final phase of my life. If I wanted to do things by the book, it was time I got to work and sent a wrecking

ball smashing through my vocabulary. I wondered if I
was ready for it.

'Do you know Bohumil Hrabal?' I asked, thinking I
should take advantage of the opportunity while I was
still able to talk a little.
    'How am I supposed to know him? I'm senile!'
    'A writer!' I continued. 'From Prague. The man was
already in his late eighties when his health started to
deteriorate, and he was admitted to a home. He's supposed to have met a fairly poetic end there, falling out
of a window while feeding the birds. But according to
those in the know, he deliberately threw himself out of
the window, piss-pot, wheelchair and all. A voluntary
defenestration, which was a little more symbolic in his
hometown than it would be here.'
    He interrupted me.
    'Watch out, you babbling idiot and shut your gob.
That fat nurse whose armpits start to reek in the morning
after she's lifted her first three emaciated grannies out of
bed is waddling this way. No doubt to snap at us that
our bus is running late and ask if we don't want to go
inside for five minutes for a cup of coffee.'
    'What? Is the bus late? I'll never learn to play the
bloody piano.'

★

I'm crossing the Styx and taking: a tube of tooth-paste (just for a joke), a stray Joseph Roth quote, the wondrous memory of an ardent kiss I never got, bread crumbs, greater solace than a good Berliner ever offered me, a stanza of 'Auntie Bonanza', the longing for a T-shirt emblazoned with the words LIFE BEGINS AT SEVENTY-FOUR, more hope than certainty that someone will be waiting for me on the other side. And that's all.

\*

Moniek De Petter was beside herself with rage when she caught me puffing away like a pro in the canteen during one of her obligatory visits. A roll-up of my own manufacture, produced with tobacco my wandering comrade had deposited in my room. And a nice glass of wine to go with it – or at least a glass of wine. It was only then that I became, in her eyes, the embodiment of mental degeneracy, even if she still thought my erratic behaviour could only be the result of excessive and clearly inappropriate medication and reserved her first dressing-down for those she saw as the chief culprits: what kind of useless doctors were they, letting their patients smoke and get sozzled? She was going to put in a complaint, an official complaint! She'd go straight to the heart of the Medical Council! And then they could hang onto their braces, because soon they'd be struck off and lucky to get a job chasing a dustcart!

'My husband's been an intellectual his whole life. He used to chat to the sparrows in the back garden in Latin to practise his languages. And look at him sitting there now with that filthy thing in his mouth. He looks like a beggar straight out of the Fourth World.'

Of course, it wasn't as if I could do anything about it; I'd simply forgotten I'd given up. A typical symptom of my disease, neither more nor less.

My daughter's astonished reaction during what proved to be her last visit was much warmer.

'God, did you use to smoke? You never told me. And now I think about it, I've never seen a photo of you with a cigarette either. Even though I've been poring over those old albums of yours a lot recently.'

She then lit up one of her own. She didn't even need to cadge it off someone, she just fished it out of her handbag. One-upmanship in the surprise department. Because that was something I didn't know: her being a smoker.

'It's a treat I'd given up hoping for, Father, one day being able to enjoy a cigarette in your presence. Well, maybe not *entirely* in your presence . . . But in your proximity at least. Still, my whole life I've kept this poisonous but very tasty habit from you and sometimes I found it hard to believe you didn't realise I was a smoker . . . How could you not have cottoned on to my smoking in the shed when I was a teenager! I did it because I enjoyed it. And more than that: those cigarettes were the perfect companion for a slightly lonely, aimless adolescent. It was either smoking or stuffing myself full to the gills with sugary garbage. As far as I'm concerned, I made the right choice. And it's not as if I didn't have more than my fair share of overripe spots anyway, without encouraging them. But I kept my smoking secret, of course, chewing coffee beans so my breath wouldn't give me away, a fairground con I can't imagine smart parents falling for. Unlike you two. I'm pretty sure Mother would have taken a swing at me if she'd found out her well-bred young daughter had lowered herself to the suicidal pleasures of the hoi polloi. She would have cursed me up and down for a whore, like she did when she checked the laundry basket and found out I'd taken to wearing black underwear. Black underwear *and* a smoker, a combination like that would have done her head in. Especially considering she'd already discovered that I'd gone to the doctor behind her back to get a prescription for the pill. That already made me the scum of Gomorrah and the first nail in her coffin. She threatened our GP with everything imaginable: he should be ashamed of himself for encouraging unmarried underage girls to get up to all kinds of perversity. That kind of thing . . . It was around then that she changed doctors. You didn't really pay much attention. You had your nose in a book and I'm sure you found intimacies like that too delicate a subject for a father to discuss with his daughter.'

Gulp.

'Maybe you were brave enough to broach the more sensitive subjects with Hugo, man to man.'

Gulp.

'. . . You see, I'd already left home, becoming what they used to call an independent woman, and you still didn't know I was a confirmed smoker. A pack a day, easy.

In the end I found it simplest to just keep the peace by not smoking on the few occasions I came round. I just had to get by on a temporarily reduced dose of nicotine. New Year and other family get-togethers always cost me my nails. And if I finally gave in to my addiction and stepped outside for a moment under some pretext, it was incredibly exciting to be smoking in the garden again. As if I'd turned the clock back to sixteen. But here I am, sitting with you, all grown-up, in the dreaded forties, at the wrong end of them, and I'm smoking in front of my father for the very first time. Absurd, isn't it?'

Absurd . . . But was she talking to me or to herself?

Just then Rosa Rozendaal was wheeled into the canteen by a kind and ambitious nurse who was hoping to break through Rosa's depression with some coffee and a piece of cake. A change of atmosphere, even just from a room to the canteen, can do wonders for a worn-out soul. And anyway why did Rosa hardly ever get any visitors? Where was her husband? Was he already pushing up the daisies? And her children, what was keeping them? Or didn't she have any?

She bit into her cake and smiled for once. They'd remembered to put in her teeth. Well done.

'You don't know who I am anymore, do you?' My daughter was talking to me again.

She sighed and once again reached into that colossal handbag of hers, a portable lost and found, and after some rummaging fished up a lighter. I couldn't refuse the cigarette she offered me.

'If only you knew,' she continued with forced normality, 'how unique this place is in this day and age. I don't know any other public space in the whole country where you can still smoke inside. But it makes sense. Try explaining the public-health dangers of passive smoking to someone with dementia, whose thoughts are way back in the twentieth century. I'm guessing you wouldn't understand just why you have to go and stand out in the cold and rain like a naughty schoolboy to smoke your ciggies.'

I was still looking at Rosa, watching the last bit of cake glide into her mouth.

When I had summoned up the courage to again turn my gaze more or less in Charlotte's direction, I saw that her eyes were swimming with tears. And with a shock I should have anticipated, I realised she was looking at me the way you look at someone for the last time. She had come here today to say goodbye! Something she'd done in her heart months ago. My true self was long gone, after all. She could no longer bear to visit someone who didn't recognise her. The only man she was willing to recognise as her father had dissolved in the mists of his own memory. This was going to be her last trip to this den of misery, her final symbolic visit, to round it all off. I saw it. I felt it. And I couldn't raise any objections. My son had chucked it in long ago.

(*'Whether I'm sitting in front of him or not, he doesn't even know who I am anymore. If you ask me, my presence only upsets him . . .'*, I could hear him saying it.) And from tomorrow Charlotte too would use those glib phrases to soothe her conscience about her premature goodbye.

(*'I wanted to remember my father the way I'd always known him, not as the complete stranger he became.'*)

Of all my pétanque buddies not one had come to visit me here. Neither had any neighbours or former library colleagues. My brother? Never! And why on earth would they? I was already as good as dead. An empty husk perched on a commode. If my daughter could no longer bring herself to visit, only Moniek would be left. My last and only connection to existence. But that too could be severed.

Charlotte talked at me the whole time, almost constantly. Not because she was counting on some kind of communication, but because it was something she would never do again. The occasion demanded it. And because we're all so desperately awkward when it comes to goodbyes.

'You've really pulled the rug out from under us,

Father, with your illness. Did you know that? Me especially, because our Hugo doesn't really let it get to him. He's too busy with work and the kids' exams, you know him. Mother backtracked on the idea of looking for a flat at first, but now she's arranged it after all. She's moving on the last Saturday of the month. She's got a beautiful place, she can't complain. In the middle of town, with everything she needs close at hand. But she refuses to admit she'll have to make do with less space and is hanging on for dear life to the whole jumble sale that's been gathering dust up in the attic for years. Dresses that don't fit anymore and will never fit again? She's taking them. And why? Because "Do you have any idea how much that dress cost?" Three boxes full of drawings Hugo and I did in the nursery class, tent pegs and a groundsheet from the year dot, something hideous made of ivory . . . It's all going with her! And it's not going to stop there. Now she wants me to trot off to Sanders Furniture Emporium with her to buy a cupboard for her tea towels. She has to get rid of some bloody cupboards, not buy more. But she doesn't get it. She refuses to get it. Instead she's pissed off with me. "You're already just as bad as your father, he wouldn't buy me a cupboard either . . ." Meanwhile our Hugo just busts his gut laughing . . . I've realised that I can look forward to quite a few years of drudgery and thankless sacrifice. At the moment, all I really want is to press the fast-forward button. These years aren't going to be any fun for anybody: not me, not you, not anybody.'

A good moment for a fart, I thought.

'Did you know Mum's already decided what music to play at your funeral? Elton John's "Song for a Guy". I can't imagine that's something you ever enjoyed listening to and, actually, just three notes of Elton John were probably enough to give you amoebic dysentery, but there's nothing I can do about it. I told her, Mother, please, that song is actually a musical declaration of love by one homosexual for another, so if you ask me it's not really appropriate for Father's funeral. But she couldn't care less. Your having dedicated a sizable portion of your life to building up a proper classical music section in the library doesn't matter a bit. Just like nothing about a human life matters at the end. Forget Tartini, forget Schubert. It's going to be "Song for a Guy" and that's all there is to it.'

A better moment for a fart, but my bagpipe was deflated and refused to blow.

A frisson of elation swept through the canteen: the young and handsome Kukident rep had been spotted on the premises.

And it was true, if you looked outside you could see his car, painted with the slogan: KUKIDENT — GIVE LIFE A SMILE! The female staff gabbled and giggled, patients were suddenly being wheeled up and down the corridors in the hope of bumping into the sales Adonis, as if by chance.

Daughter dear had fetched another glass of wine from the bar (not for me, unfortunately). She was looking tired. She'd never been a great believer in cosmetics and that hadn't changed.

'Pascal and I are separating,' she blurted after returning to our table and taking a slug from her glass as if it were lemonade.

'You're the first person I've told, but I feel like you can keep a secret.'

At least she hadn't lost her sense of humour!

'I know you were extremely fond of Pascal. He felt the same way about you. He thought you were a tiptop person and like a father to him. But it is what it is. It's not that anything terrible has been going on between us. On the contrary. He's the best thing that ever happened to me. But it's over. I slept with someone I can never love as much as I once loved Pascal. But I'm not feeling sorry for myself . . . It's too hard to explain. Maybe I shouldn't even try. But I'm better off practising first, before I have to tell Mother . . . Anyway, it's all a bit of a mess at the moment . . .'

She'd drained her wine.

She took both my hands in hers, squeezing gently.

'Dad,' she said, 'Dad, look at me for a minute!'

I really didn't know how to suppress my discomfort. It would have helped if I'd been able to concentrate on Rosa Rozendaal, but she'd been wheeled back to her room in the meantime.

'You really don't know who I am, do you?' Charlotte repeated, her cheeks wet with tears.

'Matilda!' I cried triumphantly. 'Matilda! I knew you'd come to rescue me in the end!'

She straightened her back, put a full pack of cigarettes down on the table in front of me, pressed her lips hard against my forehead, then left without another word.

My premonition was correct: she never came back.

*

Rosa Rozendaal's appearances became less and less frequent. She no longer added her voice to the memory choir, which made me change my tune too; just dragging myself to this imbecilic group activity was now a test of my willpower. She was also absent from Lorenzo's dance afternoons and didn't even leave her room for meals. No more Easter eggs painted by her hand, no more dogs called Pablo sitting on her lap.

Until finally I realised: Rosa probably wasn't here anymore! She must have failed to wake up from one of her afternoon naps, quietly and fuss-free, as befits a lady. Only to be found when Aisha came to wake her for a pedicure, or to give her a watery coffee with a madeleine on the side.

It's something I do wonder about when I see how drolly the carers step into the rooms: whether they're always prepared for the possibility of a dead body on the other side of the door. Do they still occasionally find it confronting or shocking? Or do they get so used to the omnipresence of death that, to overstate things, they just casually sweep the deceased into a dustpan? I sometimes come close to asking.

No, Rosa hasn't been seen for days, at least not by me, and I fear I shouldn't harbour any illusions on that score. She must have been discovered lifeless, and that discovery will have set a well-oiled, almost silent machine in motion. It starts with the mysterious trolley that judders through this building's C wing without the usual Exelon, Reminyl, Ebixa and other treats for hopeless cases, but filled with products that fall into a slightly different category. Among them, Aerodor air freshener, *the* deodorant spray for mortuaries, praised by undertakers and coroners alike for its refreshing hint of lemon.

What else is on the trolley, the very last to be

pushed in our direction? The renowned Swash wipes, of course, for washing the cadaver without damaging the sebaceous layer. Only the private parts see soap and water before going into the coffin, to ensure the funeral ceremony doesn't smell like a fish market. Fluff Strips are inserted to prevent distasteful leakages; a task generally reserved for trainees that sometimes provokes well-worn hilarity and revives memories of the odd dirty joke. Fluff Strips (a term I only picked up here in Winterlight) have the useful property of expanding on contact with fluids and seal off all kinds of nasty orifices. You can use tweezers for instance to shove them down the throat of the deceased when the fluids are threatening to drool out. It does happen. Cotton wool serves the same purpose but is much less effective as a sealant.

Ditch that cotton wool, the future belongs to Fluff Strips!

There's a box of incontinence pads on that trolley – even though most people here are obliging enough to drop dead while wearing the appropriate nappy. Vaseline, to impart a less morbid gleam to the lips. Make-up too, of course, to dust the illusion of a blush on that bloodless death mask. And let's not forget Kukident adhesive cream, the unsurpassed means of anchoring false teeth to shrinking gums. After all, not every family can see the humour in their freshly laid-out Gramp's gnashers popping out of his mouth in the middle of the last farewell, interrupting the pastoral muttering of the bedside vigil.

KUKIDENT: GIVE LIFE A SMILE!

Something that is no longer customary, as I recently heard the head nurse explain to a gaggle of giggling students, is to glue the eyes of the deceased shut with Super Glue. A guaranteed remedy against twitching, it used to be common practice in nursing homes, but it only took a single loved one with an urge for one last look in the eyes of the departed, and a nurse with an empty tube of super glue had a lot of explaining to do. And then they had to go off in search of a plumber or someone like that to make Grandad presentable again!

Afterwards Rosa's body would have been smuggled out through the rear entrance. Without any fanfare. And that was that.

She left before I got a chance to ask her for a dance. Before I got to shuffle my slippers next to hers and whisper:

'Rosa, there's a bus stop just outside. The number 77. Destination: the past. The Albatross Dance Hall. If you like, we can take it together.'

Not anymore.

∘₀∘

Since then I've played my role the way I'm supposed to play it: with total commitment. I hardly get out of my chair. I sit there gawking at thin air. I scarcely eat and if the staff didn't force me to swallow a mouthful of water now and then, I'd be cultivating kidney stones as big as clementines. I cry inconsolably and often, and don't talk to anyone. I drag my feet so much they've taken to plonking me in a wheelchair whenever they feel the need to relocate me. I get new brightly coloured pills. I don't care what they're for. As long as they're not too big to swallow, I take whatever they give me. Curvy Cora tries to cheer me up by luring me out of my room with a box of bread crumbs: she knows how much I enjoyed feeding the birds and ducks in the garden. I hear the doctors tell my wife I'm going downhill rapidly, she has to prepare herself for the imminent end. My Aerodor and Kukident trolley is ready and waiting.

*

The patients didn't notice, of course – they don't notice anything anymore – but there came a morning when the Winterlight car park was suddenly full of TV production trucks. Accredited journalists tried to force their way in, photographers trained their tele-bazookas on the object of their mass attention and did their best to set the scene with shots of withered residents skulking behind curtains – to the fury of the home's privacy-minded director. Not a single staff member could leave or enter the home without a barrage of microphones being thrust at their gaping mouth.

It was clear that all of the institution's employees, even the cleaning ladies, were walking on eggshells. Dark clouds were gathering and it seemed to me there must have been some kind of emergency meeting drum in the sacredness of their duty to maintain professional confidentiality. Memory choir was cancelled until further notice, the bingo was off, the staff were needed elsewhere and Lorenzo probably wouldn't be coming in to strut his stuff either. There was a media storm to brave. Winterlight Geriatric could get back to its old familiar programme afterwards.

My muscles had grown unpleasantly stiff since I'd decided to sit out my last days on earth like a slug. But now, for the moment, I was free of aches and pains. The developments inspired me and, despite my earlier resolution to no longer budge an inch, I shuffled off in search of adventure, moving at an inconspicuous snail's pace towards room 17, Camp Commandant Alzheimer's room, entering without knocking and closing the door behind me. Unfortunately it didn't have a lock.

The Commandant had just got up from his wheel-chair and was standing in the middle of the room, struggling with his clothes (he'd tried to stick both feet into the same trouser leg, a classic).

Constantly putting garments on and taking them off again – on-off, on-off – that's the pathetic Sisyphean activity of those whose minds have been so eroded by the years that they constantly think they have to go somewhere. The number 77 always knows exactly where.

The Commandant looked at me with big, restless

eyes, scratched his face and seemed to be considering whether or not to start screaming. The fairy.

'There's no point screaming,' I said. 'The louder you call, the worse off you'll be. So just keep your filthy cakehole shut if you don't mind, that'll be easiest for everyone.'

I had the impression he could sense the meaning of my words. He kept quiet, trembling.

'Look,' I continued, 'look out of the window! See that media mob out there? Five camera teams, armed with state-of-the-art recording equipment . . . Things aren't looking good for you, pal. Because you know what, someone's blown your cover! Your secret's leaked out! There's a mole in this home and he's betrayed you, and there's nothing you can do about it! Those journalists out there have been tipped off by an anonymous source. They know you're in here. They know that Winterlight Geriatric is your own little bunker! You can imagine the commotion going on out there. At least I hope you can. The last living camp guard from that foul war has left his luxurious bolthole in Paraguay and returned to Europe because he was so pathetic he wanted to die on the soil of his old dreams! The coward who ran when his comrades were executed – rather fled than dead, although he himself drove I don't know how many innocents to their death on an industrial scale. Now he's old and sick enough to no longer be dragged before a judge, he comes back. But you know what, friend, you're faking your illness and the whole world knows! You're about to be arrested! Can you picture the triumphant headlines?'

He was now walking around his room in little circles, figures of eight. His breathing was getting even more erratic and I realised that I could keep going with the same zeal. I'd struck the right note, even if it could only lead to him having a heart attack with the hounds at his heels.

'You're always the same, aren't you, with your crimes against humanity? Once the tide turns and you lose power, you get delicate. You're suddenly too ill and weak and tender to be tried and it would be inhumane not to take all that into account.'

He grabbed at his chest and coughed.

Like I said, I'd struck the right note. I had to push on.

'It's a beautiful day today, you realise that? Outside, in villages and towns everywhere, people are getting ready for the festivities. Because soon, when you've blown that last little bit of rank air out of your lungs, we'll have finally turned the last page on that war of yours. There'll be none of your scum left. Yes, I know, you infected your children with the same deranged ideas about innate superiority – the struggle against that poison will never end. But your generation, with you as its last survivor, was the worst yet, and hope-fully the worst ever, and yes, that generation has almost been rubbed out. And that's enough to cheer up any misanthrope.'

I flopped down onto a chair to consider the damage I'd done. The fear he must have seen and undoubtedly enjoyed in thousands of eyes was now shrieking through every shred of his tattered being.

It felt good, I couldn't deny it.

'In three days it's your birthday party. I'm sure you're looking forward to it. I'll be there too. No doubt you consider that beneath you. And now I stop to think about it: I'm not really keen on sharing my birthday with you either . . . What if I just drowned you in your piss pot? Does that fit your idea of justice? Or do you have a more original suggestion? What did you do with the political prisoners in the old days? You must have come up with a few entertaining torture methods that have never worried humanity's collective memory because nobody lived to tell the tale? Don't you have something amusing for me to try out now? How about I ram a fork into your eyeball until the blood spurts out, coming fast and thick? And then make you eat the eyeball?'

He was going to have a complete breakdown. It was a question of minutes before this simpleton lost it completely.

Maybe I'd gone far enough and needed to stop. There was no benefit to be had in continuing to hector him or taking revenge on someone who had already been defeated by a trouser leg. These weren't my values, even if I was rather tempted to overlook that just a little longer.

But there was more to it. Something I hadn't found easy to admit to myself at first. Soon after arriving in this home, when I discovered the identity of this infamous patient, I had begun to see his presence here as a possible exit strategy, a way of returning to normal life with my head held high. Because what if I couldn't bear living here? What if the loneliness, monotony and imprisonment proved too much for me? I could always expose the fugitive war criminal and leave Winterlight Geriatric as a tight-lipped hero! My friends and children might be embarrassed about the things they'd said during my supposed mental absence and the visits they'd never paid me, but above all they would praise my dedication. And my wife . . . well, yes, my wife . . . she has fangs: she bites!

So forget it, I was right to call it a day.

'We'll meet again,' I said, taking my leave of Camp Commandant Alzheimer, but he'd probably forgotten it again half an hour later.

★

I'm sure Moniek has been suffering from telephonophobia for a few weeks now. Every ringtone must sound like a death knell in her ears. Bad news has no respect for manners or the clock – that's why she'll go to bed with her mobile close at hand. It could be my parting shot: dying in the dead of night. But I have my suspicions that old folks' homes don't actually notice nocturnal expirations. Death is presumably determined during the morning round. And if they are unable to avoid noticing that a patient has been such a pain as to pop off when staff levels are at their lowest, they'll simply wait until the full day shift has clocked on before doing what needs to be done.

Every time the phone rings, Moniek will be afraid it's the *coup de grâce*. Sometimes her whispering premonition will slow her down so much she won't get to it in time. Doubt will set in: would they inform the next of kin by answering machine or would that be considered improper? She settles on the latter, and doesn't listen to her missed calls, trying to convince herself that news only becomes real once it's known.

But it's inescapable: in the extremely near future she will answer the phone and, to her great regret, she will not be met by the cautious voice of a telemarketer. It won't be a pollster or a country bumpkin who has insisted on dialling the same wrong number twice, but the warm tenor of the care manager of Winterlight Geriatric: 'Mrs De Petter, I'm afraid I have to give you the news you have been expecting for quite a while now . . .'

'Was it an easy death? Did he die in his sleep?' These are the kind of questions people generally ask.

Because we're keen to believe the dearly departed don't even know they're dead, at least the ones who had the good timing to exhale their last breath between two dreams. They are somewhere far beyond the end of days, still thinking they're about to get up, empty their bladder and eat a piece of toast while reading the morning paper. Beautiful.

But my death wasn't going to be easy. No, I wasn't going to die in my sleep.

I like to picture the scene: Moniek washing up in her kitchen, wearing her pink apron. She has just been informed of her widowhood, hip, hip, hooray, because her husband took a tumble out of his window while feeding the birds. It was very quick – falling always is – and they have every reason to believe he didn't suffer unduly.

That's how it could, might, should go.

While I'm at it I imagine my old buddies, bent over their boules. They're in the middle of a loud discussion about the state of play and have brought out the measuring tape to decide who's won and who's lost. And then Roland suddenly remembers the news he'd meant to tell everyone straight away but forgot for a moment because it was such a beautiful evening and he says, while the discussion of the millimetres continues unabated:

'There's something I have to tell you . . .'

Yes, definitely, this was something his mates needed to know.

'You can get your black raincoats out again because you'll never guess who's kicked the bucket this time: Désiré!'

'Désiré, Désiré? Hang on . . . Which Désiré?'

'Nah, come off it. Désiré Cordier, who else? You're not going to tell me you've forgotten who Désiré Cordier is, or rather was. After all those years of playing together.'

Of course everyone knows who Désiré is. Was. Quiet,

respectable. Former librarian, mad about books. Mad about music too; able to rattle off Beethoven's birthday on command. Or tell Schubert's string quartets apart. Unbelievable. Too bad he kept on playing pétanque like an absolute beginner. Under his wife's thumb. At some stage he got dementia and became a real handful, plundering shops, catching trains to Wherever-it-was. There was no other option, they had to put him in a home. Winterlight, I think. Where they were filming that series recently . . . What's it called again? Yes, it was definitely Winterlight. But how long ago was that, Désiré getting admitted? To be honest, some people thought he was already dead. But, see, he's been alive all this time. It's a shame. A crying shame.

'He'd only just turned seventy-four. The birthday decorations were still taped to the ceiling, in a manner of speaking.'

'Seventy-four? The poor guy, that's way too young to go, it really is.'

And everyone agreed. Seventy-four really was much too young to die. Nowadays, at least. With all the medical care available and the pills and the blah-blah-blah. And their backs started to ache from spending all that time bent over a difficult constellation of boules.

'From what I've heard he didn't choose the easiest way to end it all either. He fell out of a window.'

'Really?'

'He'd stopped eating a few days beforehand. He

138

used to save up his sandwiches to feed the birds in the nursing-home garden. But when walking that far got too much for him, he started throwing the crumbs out of the window instead. And apparently that's how . . .'

'That's terrible. And fell straight to his death? I hope it was fast at least.'

'And what makes it even more tragic: a few hours before he crossed the Styx with his box of bread crumbs, he wrote a few words on his bathroom mirror with toothpaste. The completely random words *tree, carrot* and *lamp*. Try to make something of that if you can. As if he was starting school all over again, the poor guy, and proudly practising the new letters he'd just learnt.'

'A God-awful disease, dementia . . .'

Everybody agreed, dementia was a God-awful disease. And then enough was enough and it was high time to get back to life. The discussion of millimetres resumed. Somebody would win the game of pétanque. Somebody would be determined to get revenge. Night would fall and they would say goodbye to each other, but not for long, because soon they would meet again, on the day of the black raincoats, to sit down together on their usual cold pew in church. And when they're standing together in consecrated silence at the cemetery, they can remark that it was a close thing, any closer and my body – an insignificant footnote – would have been lowered down next to Rosa Rozendaal's in what they unthinkingly call 'the merciful earth'.